Cocky

Romantic

FALEENA HOPKINS

Faleena Hopkins

Cover Image licensed from Shutterstock.com
Cover Designed by Faleena Hopkins
Published by Hop Hop Publications

ISBN-13: 978-1539411307
ISBN-10: 1539411303

You're the last thing my heart expected.

- Carrie Underwood

1

JASON

As we stroll through the renovated warehouse with club lights pulsing across hundreds of halos and horns, my twin mutters, "Apparently God decided to overlook my past and send me to heaven. MmmMmm, look at the ladies..." Pale ice-green eyes that are identical to my own lock onto me before he adds, "To think I almost didn't come to your overblown party."

As he drops his gaze to watch a thong-covered-ass prance by me, red tail bouncing, I dryly tell him, "Like you had something better to do."

On a blasé smirk he counters, "A pre-record release party? Who gives a shit? And I *always* have something better to do than celebrating your successes, Jason."

If there's one thing he'd never do it'd be to miss something that was important to me. But he wouldn't be

Justin if he didn't give me a hard time.

Amused, I shoot back, "Dick."

He growls, "And now it's time to get this dick licked," scanning my party.

Well, it's not exactly my party, but it may as well be.

With its closely guarded guest list, fantastic DJs, and people parading around in costume, this rager is to incite buzz for Simone Ross-Taylor, the stunning singer-songwriter about to explode into people's minds, hearts and speakers.

I'm producing her new album.

Like how a director guides a film to greatness, a music producer sculpts an artist's songs into something better than they imagined when lyrics and melody were first put to paper. Or laptop. Or whatever the hell they prefer to use for capturing magic when it hits them.

They're the diving board *and* the swimmer. But I move their bodies as they're flying through the air, adjusting their dives so they make the biggest splash, not the smallest.

When an artist is thinking too inside-the-box I'll light it on fire. "We need violins here."

"Violins on a rap album, Jason?"

"Fuck yeah. Right here."

Next thing they know they're climbing the charts with a new sound no one expected of them.

Without me they'd crack their gorgeous, genius heads

open on the concrete of mediocre-pool.

But we producers remain anonymous for the most part. This party is all hers as far as the world is concerned.

Fine by me.

I could give a fuck if you know my name.

Justin's ecstatic that the theme Simone chose was *Angels & Devils*. Everywhere we look are women so scantily clad they make your dick twitch. When most girls hear 'costume party' that means it's time to compete for how little they can wear without getting thrown in jail.

"God bless you," Justin smiles to an angel with cleavage so low you want to bury your face in it and search for water.

She waves at him and disappears into the crowd, eyes heavy.

"Going to chase her?" I ask, knowing the answer before he even has to say it.

"No way, and you know why."

"Too drunk."

"Exactly."

The 'angels' are really the bad girls, or the secretly crazy. The 'devils' are the good girls who wish they were bad. Wouldn't be a costume otherwise, would it?

In an all-black Hugo Boss suit with no tie, top two buttons open, I look damn good as Satan. Deep down, I'm one of the good guys. Most of the time.

My brother is wearing all white, proving my theory. Justin pretty much *is* Lucifer. His spotless white suit, matching vest and slender tie are doing their best to hide the dark glint in his heart.

Two white-winged beauties spot us and start gliding over with purpose behind their long eyelashes. Mmm. Look at them. We can actually see dark nipples through those lacy white bras. One turns around to say something to the other, but it's really just to show us her thong.

Justin cuts an evil grin. "Wanna tip a halo with me?"

I'm spoken for, which he knows.

You think he gives a shit? Fuck no.

Justin's favorite hobby — outside of hot and very casual sex — is to thwart my relationships. Or hook ups. Or whatever it is Simone and I have been doing for the last four months. He has no respect for it, whatever it is. And even though I'm a one-woman man and always have been, my twin would love to kick me off that horse.

As the pale-skinned brunette attaches herself to him and purrs, "Oooooo, twins," I shoot him a look.

"What?" he asks.

"You know," I mutter.

The chocolate-skinned 'angel' presses her breasts into my side and purrs, "Hi Satan. Have I been a good angel?"

Fuck, that feels good. Her bedroom eyes are telling me, *all you have to do is say is yes.*

"You've been a very good angel."

She rises on her toes and whispers into my ear, "Wanna set my wings on fire?"

Gritting teeth against my baser instincts – *why do I have to be so fucking loyal?* – I take a breath to turn her down. "I'm working, gorgeous. But my brother is off tonight." Turning my face I whisper back into her ear, "Or you can just get him off."

Sultry giggles escape both of the girls. I make a hissing sound though my teeth because I'm only human. Get thee behind me, Temptation.

Justin shoots me a look telling me I'm an idiot, but to them he says, "Angels, there's more than enough of me to keep you both occupied."

They glance to his crotch, and then to mine, since we're twins. I shove my hands in my pockets to hide the half-mast erection they've inspired but by the look on their faces, they spotted it.

All six of us Cocker Brothers are gifted in the crotch department. And stamina. And…modesty.

The brunette's lower lip goes puffy. "I'm not into threesomes." She walks to me and her girlfriend takes her place at Justin's side. "Don't go. If you stay, then I will." She traces down my abs and is about reach for my zipper when I grab her hand.

"Wish I could," I smirk, cock twitching despite myself as I let go of her wrist and brush my thumb down her flushed cheek. "The four of us would have had an extremely good time, and it wouldn't be the first that Justin and I shared a foursome. Or the fifth. Or the tenth." She's melting under my touch, so I pull my hand away. It's a fight against my cock's will for me to do this, but I'm after an even hotter prize. "Sorry to let you down."

Justin walks away with the chocolate-skinned beauty and smirks over his shoulder. "Suit yourself."

The third wheel whines after me, "Come back!"

But I'm already gone, looking for the most beautiful woman here. Simone Ross-Taylor. The star of the night. And my addiction.

2

JASON

Locating the tightest cluster of sycophants, I know that Simone is the center of their excitement. With a casual, disinterested expression I position myself where she can see me when she eventually comes up for air and looks over. Acting like I don't care if or when that happens, I lazily unlock the screen on my cell phone.

It's an act.

The only thing on my mind is those long legs of hers wrapped around my head later on tonight. But I'm not going to give that away. I have to play it cool. With women like Simone, the game is crucial.

I'm fake-scrolling through artists on SoundCloud when I hear, "You're so fucking obvious, you know that, Jason?"

Tensing, I mutter to the floor, "Shit," and shove the phone into my suit pocket, readying for battle. She's Simone's personal assistant and best friend, the bane of my existence for four months now. The two come as a package deal that I wish I could return half of.

"Good. Put it away," she laughs. "You weren't really looking at it anyway."

Turning my head I lock onto the almond-colored eyes of my redheaded nemesis, and instantly match her sneer. Then, to throw the five-foot-two-inch shrimp off her game, I travel my purposeful gaze all the way down her body, taking my sweet time.

Of course the bitch is dressed as an angel.

But her outfit isn't slutty by any standards.

She's in white jeans, heels, and a silky white blouse that's not low-cut. Short wings are pinned to her back, and there are white daisies gently placed on her curly, auburn hair for her halo.

If she wasn't such a cunt I'd find her adorable. But she is a cunt. And she's got nothing on Simone.

"*Ironic* isn't a costume," I growl before bending in close to her smug face. "Oh, hey Sarah, did your rock let you climb out to play?"

At my unexpected advance she recoils. Only by reflex, not by choice. She wouldn't want me to think I've gotten the upper hand. She'd much rather get in my face and fight me like a man like she's doing now. "Are you going to kiss me?!"

"Nobody could pay me enough."

A fresh sneer twists her soft pink lips into sharp points. "I wasn't saying I wanted you to, Jason. Don't get your fucking hopes up."

Smirking, I lean deeper in. "Sarah, my only *hope* is that after this album is finished I never have to see you again."

Her eyes sharpen with glee. "When I go, your lover goes with me. Bet you didn't think of that."

Fuck. She's right. I've been basking in the warmth of Simone's charms nearly 24/7 with work and play, and that joy is about to vanish from Atlanta.

My drug lives in Detroit.

Seeing my expression flicker, Sarah kicks me when I'm down. "Oh, are you going to cry?"

Of course I'm not going to fucking cry, but I do have to think of something fast to keep my fix from leaving before I'm ready.

"Hate to break it to you, she-bitch, but it's not over yet. We need to remix an alternate single of *Just For Me*. You're welcome to fly back to your cave while we work."

"Work? Is that what you call sex with you? I'd call it torture."

"Sarah, if you were ever lucky enough to fuck me, you wouldn't be able to walk for a month. And that annoying little bark you have would be a whimper. For dayyyyyyyys."

Crossing her arms, her breasts hike up and show their

first sign of cleavage. I glance down, momentarily distracted. "I'm not even going to reply to such ridiculousness, you cocky towheaded dick on feet. This is the first I've heard about an alternate remix!"

"Everyone knows you can't have just one version of a hit song, short-stack."

On a glare meant to whither me, she snarls, "Don't fucking call me that."

"While you're down there, why don't you blow my big cock?"

Sarah reels her arm and tries to slap me.

I duck.

She misses.

Grabbing her wrist I snarl, "Try using a footstool next time."

She bares her teeth like an animal. "I'm gonna tell Simone you should remix it by yourself."

"Like she'd give up control."

Knowing I'm right, Sarah snaps, "I'll think of something, asshole!"

"And it'll be mediocre."

"Fucking dick!"

Leaning in really close I growl, "First, sex…and now you're thinking about my dick?"

"I don't have a microscope."

"You'd need a telescope because it reaches to Venus."

She blanches. "God, that was terrible!"

A grin flashes on me. "It really was."

I'm about to release her wrist when a drunken male-angel nearly falls and in the process of righting himself, pushes her by accident. Our lips collide. An unexpected charge ignites in my bloodstream, and what should only have lasted a split second with both of us wiping our mouths afterward in disgust, keeps going on for four, maybe five seconds…with a little added pressure that didn't need to be there.

The kiss isn't long, mind you, and there's no tongue, but count to five. That's enough time to feel something happen that shouldn't.

She pulls away first, eyes wide as she stares at me. I'm just as alarmed. No way that should have felt as good as it did.

Even worse, the next thing we hear is the honey-smooth voice of Simone demanding, "What the hell was that?" Sarah and I jump back a foot as Simone's beautiful blue eyes flash between us. "What the fuck, Sarah?"

"Someone shoved me at him!"

Raking a hand through my hair, I mumble, "Didn't mean to do that."

3

SARAH

Didn't mean to do that...

Stunned and trying to think fast I roll my eyes and tell my best friend, "It was an accident! You know I can't stand him!"

Simone blinks at me.

I turn on my heel and storm off, because that's what I usually do around Jason. And even though I'm having a hard time breathing, if I do this then she might believe that nothing just happened to me.

Just act normal, Sarah.

Our lips were locked before I even knew I'd been pushed. And we stayed there. I felt this unwelcome, dizzying rush of tingles spread throughout my body as he pressed the kiss a little harder into me. I didn't want to pull away but I had to.

He's my best friend's lover.

Even if he weren't, I hate the guy with a passion.

So why, even with that chaste kiss with no tongue, did it feel so fucking insanely incredible?

I can take a lot. More than I dish out, in fact. It comes with the job of protecting someone as beautiful as my flaxen-haired, pop-singer best friend. But Jason has managed to push me over the edge of my fury-cliff more times that I'm proud to admit.

If he hadn't looked so surprised just now I'd swear he kissed me like that on purpose in order to win.

But he looked equally as emotionally jarred as I felt!

And he's not a good actor.

I can read him like an open book with large print. All those times he pretended he wasn't moonstruck over Simone just to keep her interested. The moments when he was equalizing the tracks while she sang and I saw his disappointment or his awe, when he thought he was hiding it. And it's so obvious how much he reveres his twin even when they gripe at each other.

Jason sucks at hiding what he's really thinking.

I hope he didn't see my goosebumps.

Fuck!!

Jason Cocker is an arrogant bastard! He's the second most self-involved and conceited man I've ever met. The first is Justin. Luckily, I've had less contact with that half of the poisonous duo. They really put the 'd' in dicks.

He has been awful to me for months now, treating me as if I'm a flea making my living sucking the blood off my soon-to-be rockstar friend, rather than what I *really* am to her — the foundation that keeps her building from falling.

I run all of her business affairs. I'm the reason she got signed to the record label — I emailed and followed up again and again. I made sure they came to her concert to see how good she really is. I book the plane tickets. The hotels. The shows in all the cities, even before anyone knew who Simone Ross-Taylor was. And I'm happy to do it because I idolize her and always have!

She's amazing.

And I just kissed her lover right in front of her.

I need to disappear.

Jason Cocker, what a jerk. He struts around like he's the only one who can create a hit album. Like his schedule is more important than the one I set up for her. Like his amazing body, perfect nose and gorgeous green eyes are so incredible they're going to make someone like my Simone change her semi-slutty ways so she can settle down in Atlanta and have his babies.

Yeah, right buddy. Never gonna happen.

She never opens her heart to any of the guys she's fucking. Not one since I met her when we were both sixteen and she moved to Detroit.

Men are to be used. She's taught me that.

Not that I use them.

Who has the time?

What am I supposed to do, juggle them between keeping her wild life on course and losing a much needed fifteen pounds that won't seem to vanish from my hips!?

It's fine. I'm not lonely. Men are not in my future, and that's alright. I've gotten used to the fact that she gets the attention and it's my place in life to sweep up the ashes she leaves behind in every city. That's what I've been put on Earth to do.

And from what I see of men, I am not turned on by their actions so it's no big loss for me to support Duracell single-handedly. Pun intended.

The games they play! No, thank you. And for God's sake, the whining to me after she tells them it's over! It's sad and so unsexy. I have to pat their backs and tell them, *What'd you think was gonna happen? Grow some fucking balls. Don't use up all my tissue. We still have a show in Austin, Texas.*

Also, I never get asked out, so that's good.

I'm saved the annoyance of dating by the sheer fact that when you're only 'average' it's nearly impossible to get noticed next to a glowing flame like Simone.

Maybe it was because of my inexperience that Jason's

lips had this vibrational effect on me.

My longest relationship was mid-college and lasted a mere two months long. It ended the night I handed him my virginity and he groaned in my ear right afterward, "Shit."

"What?"

"Didn't mean to do that."

There I was underneath him and also under the false impression that maybe I could love the jerk (I was a bit naive then), so for the life of me I couldn't understand the meaning behind his slurred statement.

Tracing his few chest hairs I asked in my softest voice, "You didn't mean to do what?"

He was so wasted he didn't think to pause and consider a girl's feelings before confessing, "Simone will never date me now that I fucked her best friend."

Sucker punch to the gently-used vagina.

The two months I thought we were dating were really him just hanging around me to be close to her. Then Vodka entered the picture and my virginity exited.

Yep. One time I had sex.

Not once *upon* a time, because that would suggest it was a fairy tale experience. I wish it were make believe. But it was very real.

And now those five debilitating words have come back to haunt me all over again.

Didn't mean to do that.

Ouch and sigh and fuck you.

I'm outta here.

"Sarah!" she calls at my back.

With my heart slamming in my chest I glance over my shoulder. Simone is following me, her white wings hitting people on the way. Even furious and confused she looks stunning in a form-fitting, low-cut, white gown, petite breasts bouncing. So many of the other women at this party went for mini-skirts or even the whorish-thong choice.

Simone looks like she could be the beautiful bride to Archangel Gabriel himself.

Me? I went for angel-casual and I'm secretly very proud of my halo made from tiny white flowers.

But next to her I know what I look like.

Invisible.

Bursting out the warehouse's back door into smoky air, overlapping conversations and twinkle lights, I stare at the asphalt beneath my heels in an effort to lay the bricks down around my psyche before she arrives. I just need a second to put my wall in place again! I hate the sudden ache in my chest, especially when my lips are still buzzing from his.

Why did it have to feel so good? What a fucking asshole that guy is!

She explodes through the door, grumbles, "Shit!" as

one of her wings rips on it and storms at me, "What the hell was that kiss, Sarah?"

"Let me get it," I mutter, digging into my handbag for a safety pin. "Turn around."

There's no hesitation on her part since I've fixed her stage costumes countless times over the years. While my shaking fingers nearly stab each other, I wrestle to secure her wing.

Over her shoulder she demands, "Well?"

"If you'd walked up a second earlier you'd have seen me slapping him! It wasn't a kiss, Simone. Some guy shoved me into him when he was up in my face! Hold still."

Planting delicate hands on her slender hips, my blonde superstar lets out an aggravated sigh. After a silent moment she mutters, "You slapped him?"

"Yep. Wasn't a light slap either."

Never really hit him because he ducked and grabbed my wrist, but that's not important right now.

"I wish I would've seen that," she smiles. "You fix it?"

Patting her back to let her know she can turn around, I prepare for the lie. As she turns on me with questions in her beautiful blue eyes, I reassure her, "The kiss was awful. Like kissing rubber. How do you put up with that guy?"

Believing me, she finally releases her ego and admits, "He's just to pass the time. I like attention. You know that."

"Why'd you get upset with me then?"

She thinks about it. "I don't know. Because I was supposed to, I guess?"

Exhaling relief, I mutter, "Jeez...I was scared I'd stepped way over a line even if it wasn't on purpose." Off her amused shrug, I shake my head. "You really love drama, you know that?"

She leans in to whisper in my ear, "No, Sarah, I *make* drama." Pulling back she winks, "It's why they pay me. I'm not boring."

"They pay you because your music makes them dance."

Simone laughs with a twinkle in her eye like I know nothing. "There are a lot of singer-songwriters out there. I'm headed where I am because I know how to entertain people. Part of that is creating heat. Drama is fire."

"Which I always have to put out," I mutter, glancing around the crowd of mostly smokers, a warm Atlanta breeze wrapping around us all.

A spark lights her eyes and Simone calls out, "Everyone!"

People turn, their conversations momentarily thrown on pause.

After a few beats of silence, right before things get awkward, Simone opens her lips, inhales a soft, deep breath and begins to sing her new, unreleased song *Just For Me*.

> *You used to say you needed me.*
>
> *But you really needed you.*
>
> *Watch me sleep-walking awake.*
>
> *Going the distance it'll take.*
>
> *To heal this weeping wound.*
>
> *Can't let heartbreak find me*
>
> *Before you come back too soon.*
>
> *Can't change my mind.*
>
> *Don't force a try.*
>
> *This is just for me.*
>
> *I need to leave the you that formed the we.*
>
> *And walk away to put the past to sleep.*
>
> *So I can have a future worth having…*
>
> *Just for me.*

It's an abbreviated, a cappella rendition and when Simone closes her eyes and goes quiet, everyone is silent at first because they're stunned.

The beautiful creature I call my friend was given a gift by God. While I know she's no angel, she sure does sound like one.

Everyone goes nuts with applause, rushing forward to thank and try and talk to her.

In awe, I'd stepped back for her to take the stage when the song began. And there's a tear in the corner of my eye.

With a sweet, shy smile Simone nods gratitude at their praise. She holds her hand up and motions for me to come to her. "Everyone, I want you to meet Sarah Daly, my personal assistant and best friend. Couldn't be where I am without her."

Blushing bright red I glance around the faces as I receive fresh applause, walking to her side. The attention is too much for me, so as Simone begins to answer questions like, "Did you always know you were going to be a singer," I turn away to disappear.

I'm much more comfortable in my usual state of anonymity. It's where I spend all my time. I like it. Hence the wall.

But as I go to hide I'm surprised to lock eyes with Jason's narrowed gaze, those pale green irises slicing into my bloodstream in a way they shouldn't be able to. I feel his presence all the way down to the arches of my feet.

Standing in the doorframe of the warehouse in a form-fitting, extremely sexy black suit, Jason Cocker holds my look as he starts to slowly clap, like he hates me.

I glare at him, cock my head a little, and give him the finger, mouthing, *I hate you, too.*

He turns and disappears back inside the party.

Staring after him, my face softens. *Now if I can only forget how good you taste.*

27

4

JASON

Back inside, one of the record company executives approaches me. "Jason, just the man I was looking for."

"Mark," I greet him with a frown, my mind on the women.

"Quite a party. My favorite aspect of my job, the groupies," he smirks, casting a quick glance around the undulating dance floor. "Perfect location, by the way."

"Gave us the space we needed," I nod, still distracted.

"So, I was thinking we promote the release with the single, *Time Doesn't Fly.*"

"Nope. We're going with *Just For Me.*"

His eyebrows rise and he crosses his arms, unconvinced. "I think the other one is more of a dance tune."

Tune? Man, I get that you're square and older than your dye-job would have me believe, but come on.

The suits behind the magic never get it. They can't. Music isn't in their blood. Money is.

"Mark, if you just heard what I did you'd know *Just For Me* is going to be huge." He looks at me with curiosity. Motioning toward the outside smoking area I tell him, "Simone just did an a cappella version of it for the crowd back there that was so fucking good I have no choice but to remix a version in that direction."

"Really," he nods, interest piqued. "She just sang out of the blue like that. Hell of a press idea. We should film it."

"You said no cameras," I remind him.

"That was before," he smirks. "Know anyone?"

"Of course I do. This is my city. Give me half an hour." I walk off and pull out my phone to call my buddy Jimmy Vay, a videographer who covers a lot of the live music events here in Atlanta. In a matter of seconds he confirms he'll be here. I nod to Mark across the room. His stiff co-executives lean in while he presumably tells them the plan.

But now I have to convince Simone. And frankly my feelings about her are a little muddled at the moment and I don't know why.

"I need a second to get my head back on straight," I mutter, alone as I watch thongs jiggling in front of me. From between them Justin emerges with his hair all fucked up. The look on his face makes me smile. "That good, huh?"

29

"Dirty little angel, that one," he smirks. "What's with your face?"

"You mean your face?" I throw back, pointing at him. "You're so fucking pleased with yourself, it's hilarious."

He frowns, "Yeah, well yours looks like you just faced a guillotine."

"For my balls, maybe," I snort, unable to deny he's read me correctly. "I have to convince Simone to sing a cappella. And I might have to go through Sarah to make it happen if she turns me down. Not looking forward to it."

"The attention-whore won't balk."

Pushing his shoulder, I warn him, "Don't use 'whore' in reference to her ever again, ya hear me?"

Unfazed he smirks, "Attention-whore is not a prostitute. It's a common term. Don't get your boxers in a bunch."

My shoulders relax. "I'm going commando."

"Me too," he grins. "Helped enormously just now." He cocks his head. "Why are you so tightly wound up all of a sudden? When I left you…"

I'm one breath away from confessing I accidentally kissed Sarah but instead I interrupt him with, "Simone just did the song for an audience, and she'll think it's inauthentic to perform it again for a camera."

He scoffs, "A hundred bucks you're wrong."

"You owe me two hundred already."

"Great, then after I win I'll owe only one."

"Get ready to owe me three." I stroll back out into the twinkle lights with him following. Simone is centered like a firefly in a swarm of gnats. Damn is she beautiful.

Her redheaded she-bitch glances over at our approach and her jaw hardens instantly. Our eyes lock for a second longer than they should and mine narrow on her. It's not easy to look away for some reason.

"Simone," I call out, all business. At my tone and mid-sentence, she glances over. "Need to talk to you."

"Excuse me, everyone," she smiles. They part to let her by, but their eyes linger. Men and women, they both worship her for different reasons.

My twin coughs. He can't wait to win.

"What is it, sexy," Simone smiles.

"Oh, no, it's *Jason* who's talking to you, Simone. Not me. Direct your compliments his way."

She throws him a look. "I meant him, Justin."

As my brother winks at her I glance to Sarah again and find her watching me in an unguarded way. She turns her face, acting like I didn't just catch her.

Back to Simone, I inhale and shove my hands in my pockets, voice deep and nonchalant as I explain, "We heard about your singing out here, and Mark wants to video you doing it again, inside to the bigger crowd. For publicity."

Her slender eyebrows fly up as her cherub lips fall open. "Really?"

Phew. She is a stunner.

Simone is the type of beautiful I fall hard for – the ethereal, waif types. Like Bernie Lancaster and half a dozen other women who've held my balls in a sling. Tall, lanky blondes that look like they could be fairies in a flower-laden forest. And the fact that Simone can sing is like pouring lighter fluid on my cock.

"And I came up with an idea for the remix where we do it solely a cappella until the very end." I pause for effect. "Then we'll have a boy's choir come in and harmonize."

That inspiration just hit as I was talking.

That's how good I am.

"Oh my God," she breathes, into it.

Sarah had been standing back, listening. At this she steps forward with that stubborn face of hers. "We have to be getting back home, Simone."

"Why?"

The women lock eyes and a silent battle takes place. Throwing up her hands, Sarah steps back into the shadows. "Fine." She locks eyes with me for a hot moment. She hates my guts. Strange kiss or no, the feeling is mutual and stronger than ever.

"I think that sounds amazing, Jason," Simone smiles, touching my lapel. "I'm so glad I thought of it."

My brother snorts.

As her eyes cut his way, I explain, "She did think of it. She sang it a cappella without my knowing she planned to do that. Hell, I only heard about it. Wasn't even a witness."

Why am I lying about that?

"Making it an actual song is your idea," he argues. "And the choir is all you. I saw your face just now. That idea just hit you so don't play it off like it was her."

Knowing the ego of music artists, I hastily deflect, "Simone's a genius. She would have come up with that on her own."

Now Sarah snorts.

Simone turns her head, making her redheaded friend drop the entertained smile.

Simone's neck lengthens as she slides her arm around mine to lead me back to the main party. She smiles at me like I'm the only man on the planet. "When are we going to film?" Over her shoulder she asks Sarah, "You did fix my wing right? You didn't fuck it up more?"

I glance back and frown. It stung Sarah to be talked down to like that as if she's some incompetent servant, and in public. Simone never talks to her that way. An odd protectiveness overtakes me as the redhead forces a smile and answers, "Of course, Simone, you look perfect."

I'm about to say something. Why I would cut my own dick off to come to that tiny she-bitch's aid makes no sense to me, but here I go opening my mouth to call Simone out. My words die on my tongue when she squeezes my arm and smiles up into my eyes, numbing my brain with her beauty.

Under his breath Justin mutters, "Won the bet."

"What bet?" she asks me and not him.

"He bet me I wouldn't bum a cigarette."

"I didn't know you smoked."

"Just quit. He's keeping me honest," I smile, glancing to my brother with a look that says *if you tell her I've never smoked a cigarette in my life, I'll knock you out.*

He really wants to tell her what he thinks of her, and that I just lied. It would make him happier than when he was balls deep in that woman earlier to get Simone so pissed that she might fuck up her performance, and then blame me. That would make Justin's whole year.

Because he hates every girl I've ever dated.

Always has, always will.

Off my warning look he licks his lips and smiles.

5

SARAH

With delicate hands on her lucky light blue headphones, Simone is singing *Just For Me* in the sound-booth for the millionth time.

I wanted to be home in Detroit by now.

It's been a week since that party.

Everyone had to recuperate from their hangovers, emotional and otherwise.

Simone needed an extra sauna day to heal and prepare her voice.

Then she wouldn't get out of bed one morning and declared it Netflix day, so I had to reschedule for one more day of hibernating in our Airbnb.

Jason came over and I wasn't allowed to let him in. That was a fun battle with her safely hidden away all comfy on the couch, he and I growling at each other on the porch until he finally called me a fucking cunt and sauntered back to his Escalade, peacock feathers flared. At least he didn't screech his tires like a child.

But still, hard-ass bitch or not, it's wearing on me being around him. He smells so good, damn him.

It was worse when I had to be alone with Jason the next day. That half hour of hell was to kick his graphic designer in the ass for not meeting his deadline on the album cover. Jason wouldn't allow me to handle it on my own.

"No fucking way! I'm not letting you damage the relationship I've built with him because you hate men."

I didn't argue that I don't hate men, because Jason can think whatever bullshit he wants to about me. Fighting with him is helpful because it keeps me at a healthy distance that I suddenly need.

Ever since that accidental, prolonged kiss my brain has been upside down when it comes to this man. Especially after Simone told me he's just passing time for her, that her feelings aren't involved.

Knowing that insider information has spawned a grain of hope in me. Which is not only crazy, but stupid, too. Even if she ditched him tomorrow Jason would never see me the way he looks at her. I'm not the awe-inspiring type.

The night of the release party they left together. At first I felt totally fine with it. It's four months now that I've watched them go, so it was nothing unusual.

But as I walked to our rented Lexus I made the mistake of glancing over as he slid his hand possessively onto the small of her back. Then he opened the car door for her and smiled with wordless, sexy promises of what he was going to do to her as soon as he got her alone. I should have looked away but I was frozen there in the parking lot, blushing from seeing what I shouldn't see.

And when she arched toward him, all feminine flirtation and how he darkened with lust for her, I felt incredibly inadequate and pathetic.

When you spend your life next to someone with her kind of unattainable beauty, no one is going to gaze at you and say, "Holy shit, look at you! You're so amazing."

No, they're going to say to themselves, "She's not as hot as her friend."

So I went back to the Airbnb house we rented and fell asleep with loneliness on my mind. And then to add fucked-up-ness to heartache, around eight o'clock the following morning I woke up aroused from a dream I didn't ask for. It was of Jason doing all sorts of deliciously wrong things to me. I was even tied up at one point and damn if I didn't enjoy it. Those pale green eyes held desire in them for the first time when they locked on me. And pleasure. He wanted me. I've never known that feeling until that horrible dream.

I woke up confused and guilty. Had to take a cold

shower and drink more than two cups of coffee to get my head back on right.

Ever since, I've been extra rude to him.

And I've totally forgotten about the kiss.

Yeah, right. Keep lying to yourself, Sarah.

At least I have a break from him tomorrow when Simone and I go to New Orleans for her concert, alone.

I need this blessed break from Jason Cocker.

We're on harmonies now. Simone's doing them all herself and then he'll blend the layered tracks. No need for backup singers, besides the choir.

She's getting worn out. I just know she's nearing the edge.

From where Jason sits at the digital Yamaha soundboard with his left hand fingers on two of the control dials, he twists in his chair and barks at me, "Will you stop fucking pacing!?"

I ignore him, like I always do.

But then he spins back around muttering, "Your vanilla perfume is distracting me."

My head swings up as he huffs through his perfect nose and slams a button down to tell Simone, "Sorry, Beautiful. Start again."

She can't hear anything unless he pushes that button.

It's how anyone on this side of the glass can discuss

what's wrong with a song without hurting the singer's feelings. Not that there's anything wrong with this song, but she didn't hear him say, "Your vanilla perfume is distracting me."

I'm distracting him?

Does that mean he hates this scent?

Or that he likes it…too much?

And here I am tingling again. Dammit!

"Tell Simone I have to tell her something," I snap.

"After she's done with this song."

"She needs a break, Jason."

He huffs again and drives two of the levers upward, reaching over with his right hand to turn a knob. There are hundreds of dials on that machine. It's impressive and daunting to look at. But here's the thing – I know how to use one of those little buttons.

The one to talk to Simone.

I reach over his arm and hit it, leaning in to tell her, "You're at over two million views!"

She cries out, "I am!? Holy shit!"

He knocks my arm away from the console. She can no longer hear anything we say. He clamps furious, ice-green eyes on me. "What the fuck is your problem? We were in the middle of the recording!"

"You're my problem, dick-for-brains! She has sung

that song so many times you're going to ruin her vocal chords before tomorrow night!"

He growls, "I want to get it perfect!"

"Perfection is fear."

"Perfection is success, Sarah." Pushing the button he says, "Hey Beautiful, let's take a break."

Her pretty blue eyes have been flitting between Jason and I, and she nods, reaching to remove her headphones.

Before she gets out here, I inform Jason, "I think two millions views and counting is a success. That video will launch the single, and then the album, all the way to number one! So stop riding her so hard because you're obsessed with her. She needs to rest up before that concert."

I'm only 5'2" and Jason Cocker is 6'2", so when at the end of my reprimand he stands, my head has to crane back to hold his glare.

He growls, "I want what's best for her, too. Now get off my ass, you little—"

Simone cuts him off with a tight jawed, "Jason!" as she walks in.

He cuts a look to her and demands, "Why does she always have to be here when you're recording? I need to focus!"

Simone blinks in surprise. "Okay, I know you two don't get along, but aren't you overreacting here?"

Jason flips his baseball hat around like he's gearing up for a pitch. "I need to be able to do my fucking job. And this one has it up her ass to block me every chance she can get!"

I dryly inform Simone, "I said you need a break before your vocal chords slash up and you can't sing in New Orleans!"

"She'll be fine," Jason snarls.

Simone sighs, "Okay. I think we all need a break." Walking to him, she lays her hand on his chest to say, "Sarah's right. I've given you a lot of takes on that song. You've already got my best work. You're just holding on too tightly to an idea."

"Simone," he groans in this hot way that makes my stomach clench against my will. "Fuhhhhck. Let me do what I need to do."

"No, Jason, listen to it while I go take a nap. You'll make platinum out of what we did today, baby." She leans in and kisses him.

I have to look away because my stomach just dropped into the soles of my shifting feet.

This is how anyone would feel if they saw someone as handsome as he is, grabbing her hips like that. Any woman would wish they were *her* hips he had a strong hold of. It's not like I have a crush on him. These feelings are just the normal responses of a straight, red-blooded female.

Keep telling yourself that, Sarah. If it's true, why did that kiss hurt you in a deeper way?

"Okay, guys," I mutter, wishing they'd just stop.

Simone pushes him off and smiles at me. I must be imagining it but there's a glint of something in her eyes I don't like. Did she prolong that kiss to let me know he's hers?

That's ridiculous. Why am I thinking it?

"Ready?" she asks me.

"Been ready."

I follow her out, but forget my purse. Turning around to get it I discover Jason's eyes on my ass. He goes beet-red as I cock an eyebrow at him and walk more slowly to my handbag.

Simone calls back from the door, "Listen to the tracks while I'm resting, okay?"

"I'll stay here," Jason answers her, his voice distant.

As I pass him for the door, I mutter, "Yes, dog…stay."

"Fuck you, Sarah."

"You wish, Jason."

The door shuts before he has a chance to snap back at me. As soon as we're outside, Simone ruffles her hair with one hand and mutters, "Jesus, thought he was going to stop at the tenth take. What's he want to do, kill me?" She pulls out her phone. "Thanks for saving me. Where do you want to eat?"

"I thought you were going to take a nap."

With her thumbs tapping away to leave comments on YouTube, she shrugs, "No, I just didn't want him to come with."

Frowning as the asphalt blurs under our heels, I decide not to say anything. There will come a day when Simone falls hard for a man. I can't wait to meet him. But from her attitude right now, Jason isn't him.

Until recently I'd been waiting for the guy to eat dirt when she drops him. Hell, I've been looking forward to it with twiddling fingertips. But something's changed. It's not the kiss or my silly dream and the tricks it's been playing on my body. I'm sure that isn't it. I think it's because I liked his idea about the choir. It's truly inspired and maybe he does have the talent he's so boastful about. I'm positive that's the reason I'm feeling protective of him for the first time.

"You needed some girl time?"

She glances to my fake smile and shrugs again. "No, but eight hours today with Jason is enough, don't you think?"

Pulling out the keys for our rental car, I mutter, "Totally. Yeah."

Heading to the passenger side Simone looks up with glee. "It's at two million, three-hundred-fifty-thousand now, Sarah!"

My eyes go wide. "Oh my God! I think this is it!"

43

Resting her hand on the roof of the Lexus she leans toward me. "Next rental car we get? A fucking Porsche!"

Laughing, I climb in at the same time she does.

As I turn on the ignition she lightly pinches my arm. "We're heading to the top baby!" Leaning back with her eyes on the phone, she adds, "And it's all because I sang on that patio and Jason saw it. Huh…guess he is as good as he thinks."

As I back the car out, I blink a few times in confusion. I knew he saw her singing but had no idea she'd spotted him in that door. I turn my head, trying to understand. "Didn't Jason say he heard about you singing?"

On a self-satisfied smile, she meets my eyes. "He just did that to cover the fact that he was watching me the whole time. He's always hanging around, acting like he doesn't care. But he's fucking obsessed with me."

I nearly run into a parked car. Simone yells in time and I turn the wheel, almost skimming its flawless side. With a sharp intake of breath my heart races the way it does when you almost kill yourself. "Whew," I breathe, staring out the windshield.

Reading my mind, she says, "Didn't think I was that smart, did you? I see more than I let on."

Why does this announcement make me nervous?

6

JASON

The next morning while I'm cooking brunch at home the door swings open unexpectedly. Into my loft strolls Justin wearing his usual uniform of expensive suit and tie, shoes shined to mirrors. "When do you leave for New Orleans?"

With a twist of my wrist I flip the breakfast-quesadilla in the air, and without losing any of the egg inside, it lands neatly back in the pan as I inform him, "I'm not going to the concert."

"Yeah, you are."

"Nope. I'm really not."

He waits until he's right next to me before crossing his arms. "Why the fuck aren't you going?"

I answer flatly, "Because she didn't ask me. And I need a break from Sarah."

There's been something going on between me and Simone's assistant/friend that I can't define. She's growing harder to ignore. There I was recording one of the best voices of our time and Sarah's close proximity to me was holding my interest more. I could hear her breathing like it was right in my ear. When she paced, her soft scent made me want to look to see what she was up to. And there on the other side of the glass was Simone Ross-Taylor crooning a future Number One hit. I knew it, but couldn't seem to lock onto the importance of that. It was like I was...

Fuck it. I don't know. I just need some distance.

As I turn my back to grab a beer from the fridge Justin says, "You produced the album. She's debuting a song from it. You're fucking going! And I'm going with you."

Chuckling, "Oh, you are?" I throw him a can of Cadence beer.

He catches it, reading the label. "This from Reformation Brewing?"

"Yep, you need glasses or something? Why are you squinting?"

"Fucking computers have been eating away at my eyes. I've been meaning to try this." He pops it open and takes a big slug.

My brothers and I only buy from local brewers when we're in Georgia, and there're plenty to choose from. Craft brewing has become the thing and we're all on board.

"Verdict?"

"Fucking delicious. I got us rooms at Bourbon Orleans Hotel."

Sliding the quesadilla onto a red plate, I cock an eyebrow at the visual. "Wait, are you saying that's right on Bourbon Street?"

"Fuck yes," he grins before taking another sip. "Location location location."

Laughing I shrug. "Fine. I'm in."

"You're dying to be near the bitch anyway."

I glance to him in surprise, mistaking which bitch he means. He misreads my expression and laughs, "What? You said don't call her a whore! I didn't say whore, did I? I called her a –"

"You're such an asshole," I mutter, pouring a good-sized glob of salsa onto the center of the circle.

"You're going to eat that like a taco?" he asks as I roll it up.

I nod through a bite. With my mouth full, I explain, "Don't feel like cutting up the triangles"

"And now I can see your half-chewed meal. Thank you for that."

Opening my mouth wide and leaning toward him, I make a noise like someone showing their tonsils to a doctor.

Justin shakes his head like he's the only adult in the room, and walks away from me.

"Concert's tonight so pack your things."

Quickly swallowing, I blurt, "Oh shit! That's right."

After listening to her song all day and night yesterday, and layering the harmonies until I fell asleep on the dials, her concert slipped my mind. I woke up needing a shower and some food. This is all I've had since yesterday.

Whenever I'm working I forget to eat.

My brother lowers himself onto my leather couch and picks up a Rolling Stone magazine. "My bag's outside in the Audi. Get to it."

There's a single divider between the bed and the rest of the room. I've found the ladies like the illusion of privacy, even when I live alone, because Justin's got a penthouse apartment two blocks from here and he comes over all the time. Has a key and never knocks. More than once he's interrupted some hardcore fucking.

Throwing jeans from my dresser onto my king size bed, I call over the divider, "Did you notice at the last BBQ how Dad and Jaxson were acting?"

Thumbing through my magazine, he mutters, "Nope. Why, what'd you see?"

Frowning at the memory of the day Jax proposed to his future wife I call over, "They were really stiff with each other."

"Dad's stiff, Jason. You know that."

"Nah, it was like how he is with Jett. There was an anger between them. You didn't see it?"

From a distracted place Justin mumbles, "I was too busy being pissed you guys didn't include me in the surprise. Assholes. Hey, Simone's not headlining right? Who's she opening for again?"

"Jager Barris."

"Who?"

"You don't listen to the radio do you?"

Justin tosses the magazine onto my coffee table and I hear him kick his feet on top of it. If we were at Jake's place those shoes would be at the door, not on my fucking table. I should start implementing that rule.

"I listen to podcasts and that's it," Justin tells me. "Face The Nation. Decode DC. Candidate Confessional. And those are just my top three. I don't have time for music."

My hand freezes while folding my favorite grey hoodie. "You don't have time for music?!!"

"Nope."

Jumping from behind the divider, I thrust my arm toward the door. "Get out of my house." When he just sits there smirking at me like, *come make me,* I shout, "OUT."

Chuckling, Justin stands, dusts off his slacks, adjusts his junk and cocks an eyebrow at me. "I'll be in the Audi listening to anything but Simone Ross-Taylor."

I lower my arm after he's gone. "Dick. Who doesn't have time for music?" As I fold more clothes into the black suitcase, I'm still shaking my head. "How are we even blood-related much less identical twins? I mean what the fuck?"

I'm so disgusted with him that I zip up the case, thinking how I'm going to ride his ass about time-management and lack of taste the second I climb in his car. I'm so focused on it I completely forget that Simone doesn't know I'm coming. Which is why I completely forget to text her and let her in on the news.

Besides, why wouldn't she want to see me?

7

SARAH

One of the bodyguards walks up to me backstage, his lips grim. "Someone wants a pass back here. He claims he produced Ms. Ross-Taylor's latest album. I told him to fuck off, but he's not giving up."

I was typing a text to Mark, telling him we're sorry he couldn't make the show, when my fingers freeze at this little shocker. I blink at the guy a second. "Let me handle him. Lead the way."

The three-hundred-pound beast crooks a finger and starts walking over to where fans are screaming and clawing to get past the ropes. Amidst the surrounding chaos are the twins from hell, their confident expressions cooler than an autumn breeze. Jason's in dark blue jeans and a hot-as-hell grey hoodie pulled over his head. Justin's got a blue, short-sleeve button up over charcoal jeans. If they didn't dress differently you might not be able to tell them apart. Both pairs of ice-green eyes lock on me as their shoulders visibly relax.

"Do you know this guy?" The bodyguard points to Jason who's so relieved to see me he's bordering on a smile.

I frown and raise my hand. Jason thinks I'm about to say *let him in,* but instead I use that gesture to announce, "Don't know him. Sorry."

Jason's deep voice warns me underneath the screamers, "Sarah, don't do this."

Justin crosses his arms, shaking his head that I'm making a mistake.

The bodyguard looks at me, because he knows my name really is Sarah.

Loud enough for the Cocker Brothers to hear me, I tell the beast, "He's a stalker, Wayne. That's how he knows who I am. We deal with him all the time." To Jason I shout, "She's not interested! Give it up!"

As I bury my head in my phone and head away he shouts at my back, "I fucking hate you!"

My middle finger flies up and I keep right on walking.

Serves him right. I know for a fact he didn't tell Simone he was coming. I would have prepared myself for the inevitable pit in my stomach and dampness in my panties.

She's been out for his balls ever since she woke up this morning with a scratchy throat. And all over my ass, since he's not been here to take the heat.

I'm doing him a favor, but he doesn't need to know that.

As soon as I walk into her dressing room, she growls, "Why didn't you tell him to stop making me sing that fucking song earlier?!!!"

Sighing, I quickly walk over to the couch where she's drinking hot water laced with honey. "For the tenth time, you are an adult. You could have stopped him if you felt your chords becoming strained."

She bends, laying her head onto her knees. "What am I gonna do!?"

"How bad is it?"

"I have sandpaper in my throat!"

A knock makes us both look over. I touch her shoulder. "Stay here." When I get to the door I lay my ear against it and call though, "Who is it?"

"Room service."

Simone and I share a look. The knob turns without my help. Mr. Perfect Face and his matching brother walk past me.

Oh shit.

Here we go.

Simone's eyes turn to silver swords, rising as though one possessed, her index finger pointed at Jason. "You!"

He freezes, confused.

Justin leans on a wall from which he can watch the scene. He meets my eyes a moment, then turns back to Simone as she snarls, "My throat is fucked up because of your perfectionism and I have to go on in…" She glances to the wall clock. In fact, we all do. Then she locks back onto Jason. "Thirteen minutes!!"

"Simone…" He holds his hands out.

"Don't Simone me! How the hell am I supposed to sing ten songs like this?! If I can't do a set for twelve-hundred people, then how am I going to do the Arena for thirty-thousand someday? Huh?! My voice is going to crack out there!"

I have to admit Jason is weathering her attack like a champ. He's very calm as he tells her, "First, my perfectionism is what's going to make you a star. This will be your last concert where you're not the headliner."

"I can't be a star if I blow it out there! They're going to laugh at me! Because of you!"

I glance over to see Justin watching with disapproving tension around his eyes.

Jason reaches into his pocket. "Beautiful, these are lozenges that Usher uses before he goes on. And Jay-Z. And Drake. They're fifty-eight dollars a roll because they're specially made by a nutritionist to the stars."

The balloon of her fury deflates as she cocks her head, takes the roll and rips the wrapper off. "These had better work," she mutters, turning away from him.

Jason's staring at her back as she pops two in her mouth and starts crunching. He glances to me. From his expression, he's not a fan of this side of her. With her in her own world, he crosses to me.

My breath hitches as he leans in to whisper in my ear, "Why didn't you let us in?"

God, does he ever smell bad?

"I think you know why."

He nods, getting it. I was partly saving him, partly her. Amusement lights up his gorgeous green eyes as he leans in, his voice almost inaudible. "You didn't have to be a cunt about it."

Heat pools out between my thighs and I blink hard, barking, "Didn't I?"

I lock eyes with him and he holds my look in a way that shimmers goosebumps down my spine.

Justin pushes off the wall and mutters without emotion, "Simone, have a good show."

She just waves dismissively, still turned away and waiting for results. She unwraps more of the roll and pops two more lozenges in her mouth.

Jason and I are watching her.

As Justin walks up he hits Jason's arm. "Let's go."

From a distant place Jason nods before he locks eyes with me again. "Sorry I called you a cunt."

"No, you're not."

He gives me a smirk that is so hot it makes my panties dampen even more than when he just lit my ear on fire. "You're right, Sarah. I'm not."

He dips out of the door first before Justin goes to close it. On a pause Justin locks onto me as though seeing me for the first time. His eyes narrow and he disappears.

I take it back. They don't have to wear different clothes to be told apart. Give him a second and Justin will show you there's a sharpness to his eyes, almost devious, that Jason just doesn't have.

I saw it as clear as that mirror Simone's walking toward.

"Sarah," she whispers, touching her throat like she can't talk.

Oh God, did he give her something she's allergic to?

Fear grips my heart.

Is the show over?

8

SARAH

"What!?" I run over to her, meeting her blue eyes in the reflection. "Tell me I don't have to take you to a goddamn hospital right now!"

She looks like she's about to faint. Grabbing both of my arms she breathes, "They work!"

"Really?"

On an excited nod, she grins, "Uh huh!!!"

Exhaling the stress out of my poor lungs I groan, "Don't scare me like that again! Now get out there and be amazing!"

Simone hugs me and turns to the mirror. She smoothes her black halter and gives her black leather pants a tug as she bangs both her stilettos against the concrete floor. "Here we go!" She heads for the door, humming scales in excited preparation.

The door almost closes on my face by the time I get

there. But I don't mind. She should be thinking only about herself right now. This crowd isn't here to see me. Hell, they're not even here to see her, but she's set on changing that.

She's the middle act, but I think Jason's right. With that viral video and this new album, after tonight she won't be opening a show for someone else again.

I follow her and hold back while she and I stand away from the audience's view, stage left, waiting for her introduction. She's shifting her weight a little, face pointed at the floor while mentally going over her set list. I've been backstage enough times with her to know the drill. But it never gets old for me.

I'm so excited that I grab onto one of the alternate curtain backdrops hanging to my left for emotional support. The announcer booms her name as I cling to it. Simone lifts her head and steps onto the stage to tepid applause.

The people in those seats came for the headliner.

Now is the moment of reckoning.

Will she make them remember her?

Oh my God, I can't stand this!

Since we met I've gotten this excited every time she goes on stage. When she first moved to Detroit it was the plays she acted in during high school. When we turned seventeen she got into a garage band that lasted six years. I was at all her crappy little house-party shows, college dances, and even that time she sang at a bat mitzvah, and neither of us are Jewish. Frankly they were one of her most enthusiastic crowds because they loved to dance.

And over the last years when she dropped those band members who were dead weight, she went solo. I followed her when she began playing smaller clubs than this all across the country and finally attracting and landing one of the best labels out there. She's worked hard. We both have.

Every time it's like I'm going on with her.

Without my knowing it, Jason has come up behind me to watch her. Involuntary goosebumps travel up my neck as his deep voice whispers in my ear, "What song is she doing first?"

Letting go of the curtain so I don't look like a weirdo, I meet his eyes, blinking rapidly. "Ummm... she'll only be doing her hits tonight. Plus the *Just For Me* a cappella as a finale."

He nods and we hold our look a moment. Simone purrs into the microphone, "There's a new song I want to introduce you to." I flip around, shocked. With a flirtatious sparkle in her smile, she adds, "Although you may have had a sneak peek already, if you watch the 'Tube."

She steps back to talk to the band. Jason and I are close enough to hear her hushed voice confidently tell them,

"I'm going to do the finale first. Hang back a minute?" They nod. The drummer lays his sticks on his lap. The audience is silent except for random murmurs of people asking if anyone knows what she's talking about.

Simone glances my way and winks at me. Or maybe she winked at Jason, but right now I don't care. I'm on the edge of my heels with anxiety on how this gamble will go.

Raising the mic to her pretty lips, Simone begins to sing. A dramatic hush falls over the crowd. It falls over me, too.

When you watch the truly gifted, something happens in your soul. It raises you up to meet what you're hearing and seeing. Your soul knows you're witnessing a special sort of miracle and it resonates with that truth.

Art clarifies who we really are.

What life is all about.

Magic.

As Simone's voice makes the entire Civic Theater fall in love with her, I reach for Jason's hand.

I didn't mean to.

It's like when you're watching a horror film and you grab the arm of the person who is sitting next to you, but you don't realize it until after someone on screen dies and you awkwardly take your hand back and apologize.

If I hadn't let go of the curtain this wouldn't have

happened. Normally I'm alone backstage.

And curtains are all I have.

Our fingers weave together without my knowledge as she sings, "*I need to leave the you that formed the we.*"

It isn't until her song ends that I realize what I've done.

Pulling my hand out from his I mumble, "Sorry."

Jason is staring at me with a look I can't decipher. "It's okay. I felt it, too," he mutters, rendering me speechless.

You felt it, too?

But then he explains, "She was unbelievable."

Blinking at him, my lips part but nothing comes out.

On a quick frown he mutters, "I'm gonna go look for Justin. Excuse me." He disappears into a jungle of levers, chords and curtains.

Behind me the band has come to life. I turn as Simone almost misses her intro to a song she could sing in her sleep, because while the audience was losing their minds cheering for her talent, she was watching me and Jason.

We lock eyes.

She turns and sings the opening lyrics just in time.

9

JASON

Waiting for the girls to get back from the bathroom, Justin and I are sitting in Three Muses on Frenchmen Street with live jazz playing to our right. The bluesy beat is a step up over the headliner who followed Simone. I usually don't produce pop music. I prefer rap and hip hop. Simone was an exception for obvious reasons. And while I can respect some male pop singers like Andy Grammer, Jager Barris wasn't Andy.

Nails cutting into my brain was what listening to Barris felt like.

But even that was a hell of a lot more comfortable than the tense conversation going on since the four of us left the Civic Theater.

Glancing to Justin I ask, "You about done tearing that napkin to shreds?"

"You about done with fucking twats like Simone?"

I lean back in my chair. "You heard her tonight and you're still going to badmouth her?"

Justin leans back, too. "Just because she can sing doesn't mean she's worth your time, Jason."

I stare at him, then slam my beer bottle on the table. "I'm fucking tired of this!"

His eyes narrow on me. "I'm a dick because I'm telling you the truth? No! Don't interrupt." He jams his finger at me. "You know what I'm never gonna do with you, Jason? Lie to you! When I say you deserve better—"

"—Which you say about every girl I date!"

"I said, don't interrupt!" he growls. "And I say it with every girl because you have terrible taste in women."

"Oh, and your taste is so much better? You date sluts and…" I seal my lips because I was about to say prostitutes, which would have been incorrect and self-damning.

Bernie Lancaster, the cocaine-addicted model I was truly in love with, became a high-class hooker in order to feed her habit when I stopped dating her. I hung around a long time as her bodyguard because I had to protect her, even if it fucking tore my heart out every night to watch her disappear with those other men.

But at least she's still alive.

He knows what I was about to say, and why I stopped.

"Jason," he grates. "I don't fall in love with them.

That's the difference between you and me."

"What's the difference between you two?" Simone asks as she walks up with Sarah just behind her. Sliding down like a cat onto her chair, she looks between my brother and me with disdain. "Because I really don't see one except for your personal style."

"The difference is—" Justin begins.

I cut him off. "—that I have incredible taste in women."

I glance to Sarah as she sits down and for some reason that makes Simone's spine lock up like someone just shoved a pole up her ass. Knives shoot out of her eyes as she stares at me. I'm getting fucking sick of it, because she's been like this with me since the dressing room. Glancing back to Sarah, her usual purr becomes a growl. "Oh you have incredible taste in women? Yeah, I saw you two holding hands, so I guess you do."

Almond-colored eyes drop down.

I stutter, "She took my hand because you were so good."

Simone huffs, "Give me a fucking break."

Justin is watching me. "Go on, keep shoveling your grave. Maybe then she'll stop digging it for you."

Simone snarls, "Justin, fuck you. You are such an asshole you know that? Why are you even here?"

That's it.

No one fucks with my brother.

I start to laugh. Both girls look at me as I pick up my bottle. "Fuck it. You know what, Princess, think what you want. I'm done with your childish, fucking fits for one night."

Justin glugs down the rest of his beer at the same time I empty mine. We hit them on the table together and rise up, with both girls stunned and watching us.

From their faces I have a feeling this is the first time any guy has ever walked out on Simone. Her gorgeous blue eyes flash. "You're leaving?!"

I bend so we're face to face, her head tilted up. "Yeah. You're gifted. We get it. But if you ever talk to my brother like that again, we're done."

"As if I care," she sneers.

"Oh I don't mean the sex, babe. I mean the music. You can hire someone else to finish that remix, and the one for *Time Doesn't Fly*, because I won't be there."

With retracting claws Simone grabs my arm. "I've been under a lot of stress, Jason!"

Tugging my arm free, I mutter, "We all have stress. Grow the fuck up."

Locking eyes with Sarah for a hot second I dip my chin. "Goodnight."

She nods.

Justin and I get the hell out of there.

After we've walked up Frenchmen Street in silence for a while I glance over to him. "What's that face for?"

"It's your face. What, you don't like it anymore?"

Can't suppress a smile at that. "You know what I mean."

"I really don't," he casually mutters, scanning the body of a woman who saunters past him. She turns her head to meet his challenge, but he lets her go.

"You were thinking something," I pry.

"What? I have a brain. I think about things. I'm not just a pretty face." He winks at me.

This time I don't smile. "Are you surprised I stood up for you? Don't know why you would be."

"Wasn't thinking about that," he argues as we ignore the double-takes of strangers passing us. People always do that, for obvious reasons.

"Then what?"

"Nah."

"What!?"

"You're not ready to hear it."

I stop walking. "Just fucking tell me."

Justin runs a hand through his hair as he stares into the distance, deciding.

"Don't make me guess."

He meets my eyes and says, "Fine. You know what I was thinking? That you picked the wrong friend." Off my blank stare he leans in. "Didn't occur to you yet?"

"You mean Sarah? Are you fucking nuts? One, she despises me."

"Does she?"

"And two, she's not my type at all."

A triumphant spark lights his eyes. "Exactly." Throwing his arm around my shoulder he starts us walking again, but I'm not moving fast now. He's just punched my psyche in the nuts. "I'm getting laid tonight. You?"

I don't even hear him.

He repeats it. "Jason. Laid. You. Me. Couple of hot chicks. Yes or no?"

Staring into the distance I mumble, "Not in the mood."

"Fuhhhhhhck. Go back to her then. Can't give up after all that work you've put into her, huh? You know what Jason, you're so ready for marriage and kids it's disgusting. Now I know why Jaxson picked you for that surprise."

Grimacing I argue, "Are you kidding? There's no way I want to marry Simone."

He laughs, "Then what the hell are you doing with her?"

We stare at each other. "Fucking her."

"But you want more than that."

"Yeah, so?"

"So why do you keep chasing bitches? You have some sort of block in here?" He punches my chest.

"Ouch!"

"Good. Maybe I got through."

He heads off with me not far behind. "Sarah and I don't get along."

"I know," he smirks. "It's very entertaining."

"Then why are you trying to plant something romantic in my head?"

From the corners of his eyes he looks at me. "It's already there. And if you don't know that, you're in deeper than you think. Your head is up your ass. I'm trying to get it out." Looking up he spots a bar. "Let's go in here."

Before I have a chance to reply he's walked up to a woman lighting a cigarette outside. She smiles. I take the chance to have a moment to myself, leaning against the building and letting my mind travel back to earlier.

I spread my fingers out and turn it over, closing it slowly with Sarah's touch on my mind.

10

SARAH

Twice on our way back to the hotel Simone has been stopped by new fans. She posed for pictures with them and said, "Tag me," before we continued onward. Both times her smile vanished the second they were behind us.

Normally she'd be floating after a show like that but Jason is all she can think about.

I know the feeling.

"Can you believe how he talked to me?"

When she's pissed those long legs of hers move fast.

Struggling to keep up with her, I mutter, "I was wondering when you were going to say something."

"I was in shock. I mean, one minute he's like a puppy dog, and the next he's telling me off!"

"I don't think he ever acted like a puppy dog. His ego is too big."

"Oh please! He was totally following me around

everywhere. Everything I asked for he gave me. He's wanted to spend every moment with me since I arrived in Atlanta! He was just like all of them!"

I wince because the part of me that wants her not to clump Jason Cocker with the rest of her cadavers is growing harder to ignore.

"You attacked him, Simone. And you told off Justin. I think that was the big mistake."

She whips around and jabs my collarbone with her index finger, forcing me to stop. "You guys were holding hands while I was right there!"

"Exactly! You were there in full view. Do you really think I'd try and steal someone from you when you're about to do your most important set yet?!"

"I don't know, Sarah, first you kissed him and now this!"

Here's the thing. I may have a crush on Jason, but I would never stab my best friend in the back. What happened on that stage was totally innocent. I was in awe of her and I reached out. What he said back there in the jazz bar was true.

"It looks bad, I know! But I had no idea I was holding his hand until afterward! Look at me, Simone! Jason would never want someone like me when he can have you! And you know me at your shows. I'm always holding onto a wall or a curtain or something! I get so anxious when you're about to sing your first song I have to grab something. This was the first time there was a person to grab!"

Her expression changes as she admits, "You do always grab onto something."

"Right!"

The battle against acceptance is all over her face. After a long moment, she softens completely. "You didn't know you were doing that?"

Holding up my hand like I'm swearing on a Bible, I tell her the truth, "I had no clue. I would never do that to you!"

She inhales deeply and runs a shaky hand through her hair, staring out at the busy street. "I'm not going back to Atlanta."

Blinking at her, I mutter, "Wait, what?"

With a glint of power flashing into her, Simone nods and crosses her arms. "He threatened to stop working on my song. Well, you know what? Watch him freak out when I leave town."

This means I'll never see him again. Holy shit. Suddenly I feel like someone is strangling me. My voice is choked as I ask, "You don't want to make sure he gets it right?"

"Pfft. He can finish it without me. All he has to do is hire a boy's choir right?"

"Right…?"

"I trust him to pick a good one."

Say what?

She never trusts anyone with anything before running it by her first.

I should know. She micro-manages my job, and I'm fucking good at what I do.

I find myself looking for the Cocker twins. Drunken strangers are all I see for blocks in every direction. This city has a liquor problem. Or solution. Whatever way you want to spin it.

When she hasn't come up for air from her phone, I struggle against a huge sense of loss to ask her, "What are you doing?"

"Searching for our plane reservations," she mumbles, index finger scrolling.

"Why aren't you asking me..."

"Found 'em!" she announces with a triumphant grin. Peering over the screen I see that she's dialing the record company's point-man. She throws me a wicked smile. "Mark? It's Simone." After a pause, she exclaims, "The show was fantastic! Standing ovation. There are seats at the Civic, like a theater. Well, it's called Civic Theater so that makes sense I guess. But I loved it. And guess what? I led with the single — a cappella!" On a flirtatious laugh she explains, "I knew I had to win them over first and then lay out my old stuff, because you know it isn't as good as the new album." She laughs at something he says. "Exactly! Get ready for a huge avalanche of money coming your way. Oh, Mark…can you help me with something? We booked a flight from New Orleans back to Atlanta but could you pretty please with a cherry on top change that for me so that our flight is to Detroit?" Meeting my eyes like she's the queen of the world now and isn't it fun, she waits for him to answer. "Sure, have your assistant handle it. Perfect. I love it!" There's a final pause as he asks the million-dollar question. Her reply is said with a voice as hot and sexy as if it were melted wax. "No, I think Jason can finish the single for me. I trust him, don't you? Oh, I've got another call coming from Capital Records. Talk soon." She hangs up as he freaks out. I didn't have to hear him to know that sent him rushing to bend over and take it up the ass with a cucumber if she wanted him to.

"Oh, you're good," I breathe, impressed.

"Don't hate the player," she grins. "Hate the game the men designed."

"But why didn't you let me change the flight? I do all that stuff."

Rolling her eyes, she slides her phone into her clutch bag. "He needs to start earning his money. And I wanted to have a little fun." On a wink she adds, "Now let's see if we can't get you laid tonight."

"What? No, I—"

"Sarah, we're in the party capital of the South. There are a ton of hot guys and I want to celebrate my night. I'm not going back to the hotel right now." She grabs my hand and virtually drags me up the street to look for bars.

"Simone, I'm not in the mood for a second one-night stand."

"Mike wasn't a one-night stand. You dated him for a month!"

"Two months," I mutter.

I never told her what he said to me, but I did tell her it ended after my virginity was given to the bastard.

"And you've been a fucking nun ever since," she smiles, knocking our shoulders together. "Enough is enough. You, my dear Sarah Daly, are getting laid tonight!!"

I release her hand as she walks to a bar overflowing with people. Cupping her hand on the window she peers in while I feel my stomach growing more queasy by the second.

"Come on," I groan. "It's been a long day. I'll have a drink but please don't play matchmaker."

She totally ignores me, but I know she heard. She's completely forgotten the hours that preceded her performance where she made my life hell. I haven't eaten since lunch.

The queen of drama always bounces back from her

escapades because they are a part of her, down to her bone marrow.

I don't bounce.

I need to lay low and regroup like all good introverts do after there's been too much excitement.

"Holy shit," she whisper-yells. "This place is amazing. Come on!"

When I don't follow her, she hurries to me and takes my hand again. "Noooooo," I moan.

"You said you'd get a drink." Looking at me she freezes and grabs my handbag. "Refresh your lipstick. You look like a ghost."

"I'm tired!" My objection is again ignored as she thrusts *Blushing Berry* into my unwilling hand. Walking to the window so I have a reflection to work off of, I apply it and smack my lips.

She appraises me and by the sparkle in her smile, I've won her approval. "Oooooh, I so need this."

Tugged inside by force I remind her, "I'm only here for cocktails!"

"Totally," she nods, pushing us through the crowd. "Cock...tails." She throws me a smile that means danger.

11

JASON

Justin mutters, "Drunk women are so hot."

I glance to the chicks he's eyeing with sarcasm just in time to see one hurl red-tinged vomit onto the sidewalk a few businesses down, the other holding her hair faster than you can say Voodoo.

My brother and I do an about-face and shake our heads. "Fucking gross," I agree.

"Let's go in here." He jogs his head to a packed bar.

"I'm in," I mutter, following him inside our fourth bar since I told Simone that I am over her. We're now both a little hammered and quieter than normal.

More observant. Less patient.

Justin shoves a guy out of the way so we can get to the bar. A few four-letter words are slung at the back of his head and I reach over and push the guy back as he comes at my brother. He goes to shout at me then freezes in confusion.

Twins freak people out when alcohol is involved. He sputters something I can't make out and don't care to. It's enough of a distraction for him to leave us alone.

At the bar Justin motions to the female bartender. She looks like she could use a drink herself. This place is fucking slammed and everyone's talking over each other in order to be heard. If there's music playing underneath the cacophony of voices, it can't compete.

"Makers Mark," Justin shouts. "Two. Neat. Make 'em doubles."

She nods and her darkly-lined eyes flicker to my face. She glances between us once more and heads to the bottles.

Those tits are so good there has to be an ass to match. I can't see it from here. Justin leans to look and turns to me, shaking his head. "Flat," he mutters.

Despite my irritable mood, I chuckle because he knew what I was thinking. Justin and I are closer than any of our brothers are with each other.

Jaxson and Jett are tight and always have been, but for years now Jett's been gone from Georgia except for special occasions. He's on the road with his Motorcycle Club, The Ciphers, fighting battles weaker people can't fight for themselves.

Jake and Jeremy always traveled together since they were the youngest of us six brothers, but now that Jeremy's in the Marines and Jake got married, their relationship isn't what it used to be, and never will be again.

Justin and I share a bond only other twins understand. Even though we're different, there's a slice of us the other holds and will never ever let go of.

And we're definitely psychically connected. I think it comes through more when we're intoxicated and reason takes a backseat to instinct.

"Too bad."

He shrugs and glances in the other direction at the same time I do. I can't fucking believe what I'm seeing.

On the table in the corner are Simone and Sarah dancing seductively, their faces tilted downward. "What the fuck," I growl as Justin and I watch.

Rising on my toes I try to get a look at who their audience is. Three good-looking but obviously un-evolved jock-looking guys are enjoying the show. Two are staring at the rising star. The third – some fuckhead with black hair and blue eyes, is locked on Sarah.

A sharp pang of jealousy rips into me and I sway into my brother from the severity of it. I start for them but Justin grabs my arm with all of his strength.

Snarling, "Let go!" I try to shake him off.

He says, in my ear, "Hold on, Jason. Let's ride this out."

Before I lock eyes with him I can feel he's in for fighting. His head is cooler and he's saying let's not rush in and look like amateurs. Off my expression he lets go of me.

I swear to God I'm almost panting as I glare at the spectacle, waiting for go-time.

They were dressed as angels and look at them now. My theory was right. The way those two are moving, professional strippers would be jealous.

Wait a minute. Sarah's face just turned enough for me to catch a closer look at her smile. It's awkward and pained. What the hell is she doing? Trying to keep up with Simone?

The bartender grabs Justin's credit card and he hands me my glass. Tapping his to mine he sneers, "What'd I tell you about your taste in women?"

"I'm over her."

"So, why are we about to kick the shit out of those guys?" he smirks before taking a drink.

Locking my eyes onto Sarah I growl, "Look at her. She's hating every second of that."

His eyes narrow and he makes a tsk tsk sound. "Looks like your girl might be a virgin. Not good. I take back what I said."

My head nearly flies off my neck swinging back to him. "Just because she doesn't want to be a fucking stripper?"

He smiles.

I make a face and mutter from behind my glass. "Oh... you're a dick. You were testing me."

His laugh weighs heavy with what's to come. "And it's so easy, too." Eyes locking back on Sarah's swaying body he mutters, "She's too much of a badass bitch to be untouched, Jason."

"I agree."

"But she hates this shit."

"Agree again."

"Sure was fun to see your reaction. Feeling a little possessive of her?"

"You mean protective."

"No, I didn't."

"Justin, why don't you lick my balls?"

"Foul," he smirks. "Ready?"

"So ready."

We down our bourbons and because we've already had many, the burn goes down like honey. I hand him my glass and he shoves them at a small guy who happened to be staring at us.

"Oof!"

"Make yourself useful," Justin tells him, and we take off.

12

JASON

There are at least twenty people we have to shove out of the way to make a path.

The guy leering at Sarah stands up and starts to dance, but since he's standing on the floor and she's on the table, he's at the exact height of her crotch, staring right at it. Freaked out, she backs away and loses her balance, falling backward off the table where she can crack her head open.

I catch her just in time. "Whoa now," I snarl.

Reflexively her arms go around my neck and her eyes lock onto mine in shock. She's fucking wasted, all blurry and confused by my timely appearance. Within a fraction of a second the realization that I saw her dancing launches into her, clamping her mouth shut as shame flashes across her face.

"Hey, thanks, man," the black-haired guy who's about to die says.

I set Sarah carefully down because her trembling legs don't want to hold her up. "You got this?" I ask her.

She nods.

It's noisy and Simone's so drunk that she didn't even notice her dancing partner vanished.

Justin's waiting for my lead.

I tap on Simone's gyrating ass to get her attention. I know this was her idea. Gifted or no, this girl is dead to me.

As she turns around the black-hair fuckhead starts for Sarah.

"Jason…" Justin snarls.

I turn just in time to punch the guy before his hands lock onto Sarah's hips.

He reels back and does a dog-after-a-bath head shake, staring at me. His eyes shift to fury and suddenly as if they're one person, the two guys who were sitting down watching Simone rise up to get into the action.

Simone shouts, "Jason?!!"

She's just realized I'm not a mirage.

Justin clocks one of the guys while I punch the black-haired one, then turn and hit the third. The fight gets gruesome quick because other guys itching for a brawl for no reason except their testosterone demands it, jump in, some on our side, some not.

"Get back!" I yell to the girls as I throw punch after

punch, dodging and weaving and taking on whatever drunken slob comes at me. Simone and Sarah push their backsides into the crowd behind them to escape the building eruption of fists.

I feel a punch in my side and grab the guy around his neck to headlock him, slamming my knuckles in his chin while he grunts. Someone grabs me from behind to pull me off the guy and I resist. Then I feel women's heels flopping against my hips. I look back to discover that Sarah has jumped on the guy's back and is slapping his head, her little legs flailing and hitting me. He swats her off him and she falls down. I try and go for her but Simone shouts, "Jason!" pointing behind me.

I feel a punch to the back of my head.

It's not the first time that's happened, so I don't go down. Reeling around and bending, I take the guy to the floor by wrestling him at the waist and knocking his legs off balance with my foot hooked around the back of knee. His tail bone smacks hard onto the ground and he shouts in pain. I clock him in the head.

Rising up I grab a guy off my brother while two guys fight each other behind me. Justin's punching one huge, bearded guy while another is trying to make him pass out by choking him from behind. I take that guy down in three punches. As he goes unconscious he releases my brother's neck. Justin knees the bearded guy in the balls, then elbows him hard, cracking his nose open.

Justin gasps for air and locks on me.

"Thanks."

"No problem," I growl, waving the girls over with my hand, shouting at them, "Come on!"

Justin and I make a path for them by fighting our way through.

Simone screams. Even over a bomb detonating I'd recognize that voice. I flip around and see one of those guys she was dancing for earlier is now carrying her off. Sarah's smacking the guy's back but he's not feeling it. His mind is set. He has what he wants and he's not going home without it.

Sarah's wild-eyed, yelling, "JASON! HELP!!!"

I have to shove past and punch people to get over there. He's made some distance and the place is in riot mode. When I finally reach them I hit the guy so hard both he and Simone topple over.

Justin leaps and grabs Simone. I kick the fucking asshole who tried to kidnap her to the ground.

Sarah grabs my bicep. "Look!" She points the way to where people are so distracted by battling each other they've unwittingly left a narrow path between them and the bar.

I grab her hand, lacing our fingers tightly together, as

Justin carries Simone.

She's curled into his shoulder, shaking with sobs.

Checking on Sarah I glance down to see her chin set in brave determination. Her eyelashes rise and almond-colored eyes lock onto mine.

"You okay?"

She squeezes my hand and nods once. "Yeah."

I tighten my grip and push a guy back with my other hand. He was about to crash into us. "Let's get you out of here."

13

SARAH

The side door of the bar has shut behind us, muting the violence within as the cool night air comforts me.

Justin sets Simone down and pushes tear-soaked flaxen hair away from her face. "Can you walk?"

On a sniffle she nods.

Radiating anger, Jason releases my hand and storms over to her. "What the fuck did you think you were you doing in there?! You didn't know those guys! You and Sarah could have been hurt! If we hadn't come in—"

"—Just stop." She pushes him with one hand and walks away from us.

The twins are bloody and their clothes are a wreck. I'm so grateful to them I can barely think.

Muttering, "I've got this, guys," I catch up with Simone.

She's blinking heavily, trying to stop the crying.

Slipping my arm around her, we walk onward in silence while the brothers remain behind us, bodyguards determined to protect us from harm. It's very late and this is when the crazies come out to play. We just found that out. I'm having a hard time coming to terms with what just happened.

The early part of the night is kind of a blur. Right before Jason and Justin showed up I heard the guys saying something about a gang bang. But she had talked me onto that table and I was off kilter when I heard their plan. Out of my element.

I guess I didn't really take their gang-bang comment seriously, either. I thought they must be joking around, because the idea was so foul and ridiculous to me it didn't register as a possibility, or as something I should protect us from. I felt fear start to nag but everything was moving in slow motion. The many vodka-cranberries had clawed into my brain, making mush of everything I felt and knew.

Then I lost my balance and was suddenly in Jason's arms, like something out of a dream. I couldn't understand how he got there. The look on his face was horrible. What must he think of me? Does he think I'm easy? Because I'm not and I want him to know that dancing for strangers is not like me at all. I hated every second of it. I just wanted to feel attractive, so I went against who I really am.

I bet he thinks I'm…

Sarah, what are you doing with this mudslide of thoughts about him? He's off limits. The way he handled himself in there was amazing. He's like a superhero and so out of your league.

Jason is not a superhero.

He's just a man.

Stop it.

Glancing back, I meet his eyes for a brief second and feel my heart skip as he locks onto me. With my stomach sinking I turn back around.

He saved Simone, not you. He cares about her.

She's the one he just yelled at. You only get that furious when you care.

It's her he wants. And you need to let this go.

Glancing over my shoulder again I meet Jason's eyes. He's already staring at me and his face is all bruised up. There's a volcano brewing in him and it's gonna blow soon.

Justin's walking with his eyes on the sidewalk, just as bruised up.

They really took a beating for us. And they gave worse than they got. Watching them kick the shit out of everyone within reach was scary and more than a little hot.

I turn back to watch where we're going since centuries of tree growth have sprung roots through the sidewalk and our path is not smooth. Tightening my hold on my friend, I whisper, "You okay?"

"I'm sorry," she trembles.

"You didn't know those guys would be like that. You were just trying to have fun. I should have been more vigilant. It's my job."

A sniffle escapes her and she burrows closer into my side.

I call back to the twins, "Let's get an Uber."

Justin mutters. "Fuck that. I only use Lyft." He pulls out his phone and we stop walking. Simone and I turn to wait, huddled together. Her liquid blue eyes slowly rise to meet Jason's glare. I watch him soften under her wounded gaze and I can't deny that my heart squeezes in disappointment as he takes his hands from his pockets and comes to her.

"You okay?"

"Yes," she whispers, the picture of feminine vulnerability. And so unlike me.

He licks his lips in thought, frowning as he nods. "Good."

"Thank you for saving me," she says.

He glances to me. To protect myself from the feelings swarming inside I steel my eyes at him. It's a look I've given him a million times – complete disdain. He blinks at me and straightens up, glancing back to Simone before returning to his brother.

Justin tells us all, "They'll be here in two minutes," his voice deep and emotionless. He moves his sore jaw around and stares off at the cars, waiting.

Jason exhales through his nose, fading away into thought, too. Simone closes her eyes and lays her head on my shoulder. This movement in his peripheral vision makes Jason look over at us. He lingers on me a moment. A new frown pierces his brow before he looks away.

I wish so much that I could go back in time. Not just to before I said yes to getting on that table. Not even to before I said yes to all those cocktails when I knew what I really wanted was to lay my head on a pillow to make this day disappear. No, I want to travel back to before the night when that up-and-coming rap star told me about this great music producer he'd met in Atlanta.

If I could, I would steer Simone away from the club she was performing at, right after she sang her last note. I'd avoid shaking that guy's hand and giving him my card so he could email me Jason Cocker's website.

That way none of this would ever have happened. And by 'none of this' I mean the ache in my chest I'm having right now as I stare at Jason's bloody hand, wishing mine was still in it.

Lyft's infamous bright pink mustache on the approaching Prius's dashboard has Justin waving for the driver to come to our side of the street. Other drunken people are attempting to claim the car but Jason shouts at them, pointing at his face, "You really want to fuck with us?"

They back off. On alert, the driver bends to look at our group. If Simone and I weren't with the twins there'd be no way he'd let the two of them inside his spotless car. But she's red-eyed and he quickly U-turns over, rolling a window down to ask, "Everything okay?"

"There was a fight. We need to get the girls to their hotel," Justin tells him.

"Of course. Good thing you guys were there," he says, correctly reading the twins as heroes since Simone and I are not trying to escape and are clearly shaken.

Our hotel is not far, turns out. Before I even have a chance to enjoy sitting down, the silent car is pulling curbside. Simone and I climb out and Jason slides over. As I go to close the car door I mutter an embarrassed, "Thank you for what you did back there. For saving Simone." I go to close the door but he stops it with a straight arm. His familiar stubbornness is staring back at me.

"I didn't save her. I saved *you*."

My lips part and he holds my look a moment before closing the door. The driver pulls away and I watch Jason turn to Justin to say something I can't hear.

As the taillights get consumed by the darkness Simone

calls after me in a small voice, "You coming?"

"Yes," I answer, pulling away from their departure.

"You got the key?" she mumbles.

"Of course." We trudge up the steps with me digging through my handbag for the plastic card the clerk gave me.

Simone sighs, "What a night."

"Yeah…" I whisper, my mind on Jason's cryptic words.

I didn't save her.

I saved you.

She glances to me. "You can't find it?"

"Oh. Sorry. Forgot I was looking."

She nods and whispers, "Yeah, I'm in shock, too." The sliding doors open for her and she walks through. But I stop a moment and stare off down the street, the Prius long gone now.

I didn't save her.

I saved you.

"Sarah!" she calls over her shoulder.

With the key finally in my fingers I run in. "Sorry. Coming!"

14

SARAH

Simone groans, "Oh God, close the curtains!"

Morning light is streaming over our faces in the queen size bed we shared. Since we were booked to stay here just the one night we opted to save money. I tend to hog the covers so they're mostly on me and she's sprawled out in her panties plus the blouse she wore last night.

"You stink," I grumble into the pillow.

"So do you," she chuckles then holds her head and says, "Ow!!!"

"Alcohol is oozing from our pores."

"So gross," she groans. "Close the curtains."

Sighing I flop off the bed and trudge over, pulling the cord violently to the left. Blessed darkness descends upon us and all is right in the world again. Crawling onto the bed in my favorite oversized t-shirt and cotton panties, I release all of my muscles and collapse atop the comforter because I'm hurting too badly to lift and crawl under it.

My face is smooshed as I ask, "What time is it?"

Her snoring is my answer. Guess those curtains did their magic quickly.

Thanks to the pounding in my skull sleep eludes me. It's punishment meant to dissuade further forays into cocktail-city. I silently vow never to drink again. I will forget this promise just like the other times. But I like to live in denial sometimes, just like everyone.

Slapping the nightstand I blindly look for my phone. My fingers touch the tip of it, which makes me feel like I've won the lottery since I barely had to move to find it. My arm has never been this heavy. Squinting at the screen I see it's 10:37 a.m. before I drop the phone by my head and try to will the heartbeat in my brain to go away.

"Stop it," I grumble to the pain. Suddenly I shoot up in my bed so fast that I grab my noggin with both hands and cry out in agony.

Simone squints at me, "What? God!"

"We have to go to the airport!"

She mumbles into the bed, "Our flight isn't until 5:00 p.m."

"No! Remember, you changed the flights? Remember talking to Mark before we fell asleep?"

She peers at me with one eye. "No."

"Well, you did. He called you and said the new flight for Detroit was for 12:30 p.m. and that's only two hours away. We have to be all the way over to the airport an hour prior."

She rolls her head away from me. I'm just looking at a blonde rat's nest now. "We have all our shit in one carry-on. We can get there later."

"Oh fuck," I groan, climbing out of the bed and hitting the keys of the hotel phone.

"Front desk, good morning!"

"Questionable. Listen, do you have Advil?"

"We have Tylenol."

"No. I need a blood thinner and I need it now. My head is going to explode."

"Let me check." Hold-music comes on and then vanishes at her return. "I found a sample pack at the bottom of my purse."

"I fucking love you!"

She laughs. "I'll send it up."

"Great. Thank you!"

I've been in enough hotel rooms to know they see which room is calling before they pick up. This gives me relief to know that help is on the way.

"Simone!" I cry out, rushing into the bathroom. "Oh no you don't! You always do this. We are not running through another fucking airport!"

An hour and fifteen minutes later we are running through another fucking airport.

"Out of the way!" I shout at a family of seven whose pace is making dying snails jealous.

They don't hear me so I leap over one of their rolling suitcases.

And fall flat on my face. "Shit!"

Simone starts laughing at me, running with our suitcase clattering behind her. She was able to get through the slender space their pause made.

"You okay?" the mother asks me, aghast.

"Totally. Happens to me all the time," I mutter, scrambling to get my things back in my handbag. I meet the eyes of a young boy whose grin is absolutely adorable. To him I mutter, "Hi cutie!" He waves at me and I take off.

At the gate a line of nearly two hundred people are boarding. Panting, Simone and I check our boarding passes for the seats and freeze. "He got us First Class," she whispers, holding hers up.

I offer mine up for her to see, too. "Holy shit."

She grins and makes a loud whoop noise, then grimaces and holds her head. "Do we have time to go back to that store we just passed for more drugs?"

I'm blinking from the line to my boarding pass, then

back to the line. "We're in First Class, baby, they can't leave without us. Stay here." Smoothing down my hair I saunter to the woman scanning the passes and ask, while pointing to Simone, "We're in First Class. We're also incredibly hungover and need Advil. Can you wait for us?"

The tight-bun, tight-lipped, tight-everything'd woman glances to me like she hates her job. "The plane doesn't wait for anyone."

"Come on! Have you never been here?" I'm pointing at my head.

She sighs, "You have time if you run."

I shout to Simone, "Run!" and take off after her.

Now we're laughing our asses off, the rolling suitcase thump-thumping along in her hand.

There's a huge line of people buying magazines, paperback books, water and those neck cushions we all seem to forget we need until the last minute.

Simone and I rush around looking for our treasure and shout when we find it. I swear I've never had this much fun in a convenience store in my life.

We rush to the front of the line and simultaneously beg and plead to cut in front.

Simone is giving the batty-eyelashes.

I'm sticking my amble chest out maybe for the first time in my life.

Our ridiculousness is infectious.

"Hey, weren't you that singer at the Civic last night?" a woman asks.

Simone beams, "Yes!"

"You were incredible! Let her go ahead!"

"Oh, thank you!"

The guy who was about to be rung up steps to the side and we shove the package o' pills at the checker and both say at the same time, "Thank you so much!"

This sends us into more laughter. The checker makes a face like she thinks we're a little drunk still. And maybe we are. But who cares because we have a plane to catch!

"Let's go!" Simone shouts, handing over the pills and change while she grabs the suitcase.

As we're running back to our gate I've got two hands full and my purse is bouncing off my shoulder. There are only three people left in line when we jump into it, panting like crazy.

Simone holds her boarding pass out to be scanned and side-eyeballs me with a huge smile. "Aren't you glad we showered now?"

Laughing, I admit, "For so many reasons."

The seats in First Class are amazing. We have two next to each other, spread out and with tons of legroom. No one is beside us. Before the plane even begins to taxi down the runway a flight attendant who loves mascara a little too much, asks if we would like wine or a cocktail. Simone and I hold her look and shake our heads.

"Water would be great," I tell her while thrusting out my palm. "We have to take these."

Simone starts giggling and I grin at her as the woman heads away.

When the plane starts moving I look behind us and see the cramped quarters of Coach Class. Simone is looking at her phone when I lean to whisper, "I feel bad being up here."

Her blonde eyebrows twitch. "Why?"

"Because it's so much more comfortable, but we're all going to the same place."

Scrolling through social media and hitting 'like' on people's tagged photos of last night, she mutters, "I've earned it."

The flight attendant returns with ice-cold water and smiles, "We're about to start our ascent so hold onto these."

Nodding I hand Simone hers and give her a couple pills. We both down 'em and she goes back to her phone.

"I just think," I continue, "there should be an airline that makes all the seats like these and offers it to everyone. And doesn't charge for baggage. Or food."

Simone doesn't hear me. She's frowning and her mind is somewhere else completely.

The plane starts to pick up speed. I close my eyes and press my head into the cushion as we lift off. I always do this, every time I fly. I'm in a huge chunk of metal that is somehow flying above Earth with us in it. It's so strange that we take that for granted. I never want to.

"Huh," Simone mutters.

"What?"

"I just realized that Jason hasn't called me. Or texted."

With all the drama of the morning I'd had a delicious respite from thinking about him. Now that's gone and my stomach's queasiness takes on a new tone. "He hasn't?"

"No," she whispers. "I've even checked Facebook."

Frowning at her, I ask, "Is he on Facebook?"

"Yeah. But he rarely posts. Just work stuff. Still...I thought he might contact me there."

"Why, when he has your number?"

She blinks to me. "I don't know. I guess I'm just searching." Holding my eyes, she says, "Do you think he's mad?"

"Are you kidding?" Off her blank stare I remind her, "You blew up at him. Then he caught you dancing for other guys. And he got into a bar fight to save you."

I didn't save her.

I saved you.

Stop it...

"So you think he's mad," she whispers.

It's like I'm speaking Japanese. This would be the time for me to smack my own forehead but I don't dare damage the goods further. "Yes. I think he's mad. And by the way, we're not going to Atlanta right now. Remember?"

She turns to the window as if the clouds below us will tell her what she's done "Well…"

When she never finishes the sentence I nudge her, "Well what?"

Her eyes flash to me. "He brought this on himself. And what do I care if he calls me?"

"Do you care?"

"No!"

"Simone…"

On a deep frown she mutters, "I don't care. It's just…I'm irked."

"Irked? That's pretty funny."

"Well, he works for me and he should be fucking calling me. We've been having sex for months. Right? He should be calling me."

I really don't know what to say because for as long as I've known her, Simone has never had a guy drop out first. She always dumps them.

I didn't save her. I saved you.

That's what he meant. He's over her.

And he saved me because he now sees me as a friend and I was in a desperate situation. Although there's no way he would have left her alone with those guys.

It's very confusing.

Glancing to her I see a deep frown on her face as she tries to close her eyes. Worry sinks into my heart.

Someone telling Simone 'it's over' has never happened. Not once. And sure, we all go through heartache. It's a part of life. It helps us grow.

But now is not a good time.

She's about to approach some very big things in her career and she needs to be at prime performance level. She's worked too hard to have some guy fuck that up for her.

Listen to yourself, Sarah. You're like a coach or trainer or something. This is your mind talking, not your heart or your gut. You know Jason isn't just some guy. He's kind of the most amazing man you've ever met.

Shut up. It's not about me. I'm just here for support. This isn't my story. It's hers.

I hope he doesn't break her heart.

15

JASON

Pointing I tell Justin, "Look!"

Simone and Sarah are running while laughing hysterically from the airport's store toward the gates, and they don't see us.

We stop walking, our suitcases frozen and waiting for our command. "They're in a good mood," he mutters before glancing to me. "You going to call out to them?"

"Nah. Let's follow 'em."

"It's a big unfortunate coincidence they're on the same flight to Atlanta," he grumbles. "I should have booked the later one."

"Nice to see them laughing after the way we left them last night," I chuckle, their laughter infectious.

"Wait – what gate are we at?" Justin asks as they turn before we expect them to.

"A-14."

"That's A-7. Look."

"What the hell?" I mutter as I read the sign he jerked his chin at. We pick up speed as Simone hands her pass to a Delta employee who's not impressed by anything today. Sarah laughs harder at something Simone says and they walk quickly into the tunnel to catch a flight that's not ours.

Justin and I stop in front of the gate and read the sign: Detroit.

My eyes dart back to the tunnel where I can see them for a second longer. Then they vanish.

"Hang on," I tell my brother. Pulling my phone out I almost dial Simone but my thumb just hovers.

Watching me, he reminds me in a low voice, "You haven't called her today."

"Nope. Didn't want to." I meet his eyes. He nods like he's okay with that.

Frowning, I dial her record company's point man. He'll know what's going on. When he answers I launch right in. "Mark, Jason. Simone's going back to Detroit?"

He sounds like he's on his computer and multi-tasking. "Yes, had me change her flight. She didn't tell you?"

"We're supposed to be listening to choirs this weekend. I've made the appointments, and one is at a church that wouldn't let us have a private audience. It's our only shot with them, to be there on Sundays during Mass."

"That's okay. Go check 'em out. Simone said she trusts you. And so do I. I've gotta let you go, Jason. I have Drake on his way in and I need to get his numbers together. My assistant ate bad shrimp last night."

"Oh that sucks. I'm sorry. Tell him I said hello."

"You know Drake?"

"Tell him, 'Miami with Jason and Justin Cocker,' then watch his reaction."

Mark chuckles, "Will do."

I hang up and face my brother. "She ditched me."

"Good," he mutters. "Let's go to our gate."

"No, Justin, the song! She ditched the song. I'm supposed to do it on my own."

"Which you can do in your fucking sleep. Come on."

As he starts to walk, I grab his arm. "Of course I can, but that spoiled brat is doing this to get at me." I jam a finger in my head. "She doesn't understand I don't play games like this."

"Since when?" he smirks.

"What the fuck are you talking about?"

"Bernie Lancaster," he reminds me, leaning in like I should remember that.

"For the millionth time I loved Bernie. And I didn't play games with her. I was open and –"

"— you got your dick kicked into your throat for it.

Over and over." His eyes grow somber as he adds, "And you almost lost everything for her. Remember the intervention?"

Our brothers rallied around me when Justin told them I'd gone deeply into cocaine during that love affair. Bernie and I were head over heels for each other. The only problem was the gorgeous model loved white powder more than me, and she was an addict. I'm luckily not cursed with that gene. I can stop. And I did. She didn't, and turned to hooking in order to fund her sickness. I stuck around for as long as I could hack it, to protect her. I finally gave up.

I've only seen her once since then. She'd gotten herself into a worse situation that landed her in the hospital, then thankfully jail where she could think and maybe start over. Don't know where she is now and I don't want to know. A man can only take so much.

And my brother can take less.

"Of course I remember it. This isn't that. I'm not in love with Simone. And I don't play games. Didn't then. Don't now. Everything I did back then was fucked up but it was me trying my best to be with her."

"And you don't want to be with Simone?"

"No."

"You didn't make that clear last night."

"Yes, I did."

He scans me and leans back on an exhale. "So, what

are you gonna do?"

"I'm dropping the song."

His eyebrows shoot up. "You're what?"

"I'm done. She can have someone else finish it. All of it. Fuck it. Not just the song, the whole album."

"It's your album! Your name has to be on it, Jason!"

"If it is, fine. If it isn't, I don't give a shit anymore. I'm over it. We're done. I'll never work with her again."

As the gate numbers pass us we're silent. When we get to ours Justin asks me, "What about Mark and the label? How's this gonna look?"

I snort, "Are you kidding? My reputation can weather this blow. You don't listen to music so you may not know this, but I've got friends in high places."

He smirks at me. "Jason, I just give you shit, but I've listened to every single one of the albums you produced."

Thunderstruck I stare at him, lips parted. A profound love for him overwhelms me and I drop the suitcase to give him a bear hug. He laughs and hugs me back before pushing me off. "Okay. Enough."

I smack his chest with the back of my hand and shake my head. "Thanks man."

"I wasn't going to ever tell you," he admits, a devilish spark in his eye.

I give him a crooked grin. "I'm glad you did."

We start for Delta's flight to Atlanta and bypass all the people flying in Coach. As the attendant takes our phones and scans our emailed passes, I grin to Justin, "Now if you could convince Jett to listen to them."

"He'd sooner sell his Harley than do that."

Taking the phone from the attendant, I chuckle, "So true. Fucking asshole." To the lady, I smile, "Sorry. We're just talking about our brother. He's a badass. So I can call him bad names."

She smiles but her eyes have a question behind them. "What happened to you two?"

I frown, not sure of what she means at first. Then it dawns on me and I point to my face. "Oh, the bruises?!" I jog my thumb at Justin and tell her, "He said I was too good looking."

Justin cracks up, shaking his head. "And he was." He winks at the lady.

We head into the tunnel for our cushy seats and free booze.

The Cocker family comes from old money and we always fly First Class. There was one period of time that was nearly my undoing. It was when I was going through that shit with Bernie and I almost lost my shirt to cocaine in an effort to keep up with her, and give her what she really wanted. I was broke. Among other luxuries I lost was First Class. I had to take Coach for the first time, and often. I hated it, which was a good thing. It made me work harder to never have to be cramped like that again. The thing about money is, if you don't have enough you've gotta make more until you do.

It's not about spending less, it's about making more. There are tons of ways to do it in this modern world, making a living off your skills using the Internet. That's what I did. When my reputation went up Bernie's nose in the shape of white powder, I struggled to find ways to get back on track.

I'd make an extra fifty here, an extra hundred there. It adds up. Producing artists who didn't have more in their budget kept me moving forward. It turned out some of them were connected to more established artists and labels. My discounted rate led to higher-income opportunities I couldn't have predicted.

I did my best and after a while word spread.

Some top-name artists I'd worked with in the past heard I'd quit the partying life and they hired me again, gave me another chance.

I will never be that fucking broke again. But I'm grateful I fell to the ground so I could learn how to get up.

Samuel Goldwyn said, "The harder I work the luckier I get."

Truth. Truth. And more truth.

As the MD-90 begins to lift in the air, I close my eyes

and press my head into the cushion until we level off.

Feeling Justin's stare, I glance to my right. "What?"

"You still do that. You've been closing your eyes on takeoff since you were a kid. It's adorable."

"Fuck you," I smirk, glancing to my phone.

"She can't call. Stop staring at it."

"I'm not staring at it," I lie, sliding it beside my leg.

"Which girl are you looking for in that thing?"

I meet his look, my voice deepening. "You know which one."

His crooked grin appears and he gives a low whistle. "You are so fucked." Sipping Jack Daniels over ice, he goes back to the window. "See those clouds? Your heart's always been right there. I wasn't born with that."

"What'd you mean when you said I didn't make it—"

"—clear last night? I meant Sarah thinks you still want Simone. And like I said, you're fucked. Because those two are a pair, almost as much as we are. And you know nobody's breaking us up."

I stare at him and he nods a little. His eyes have an uncharacteristic weight to them. "Sarah's not the type to fuck over her best friend to be with you."

"I wouldn't want her to," I mutter, giving him a dirty look. "Come on."

"Well, Simone would. You know it's true. But Sarah

wouldn't do that, and that's what you'll be asking her to do if you pursue her."

"You told me to pursue her!"

"I did," he nods. "Before they left for Detroit. Because I dislike Simone enough not to give a shit if her precious ego gets bruised. But now, it's smarter to just let them both go."

After he turns back to the window, sipping his drink, I stare at the back of the seat in front of me, the small screen dark. I can see my reflection warped in it, and the discoloration plus cuts around my nose and lip.

My mind travels back to Sarah in my arms when I caught her, how she looked up at me like I was a miracle.

Then further back to when she leaned over me to buzz that button and force Simone to stop singing. Her smell and the electricity coming off her body made me angry because I couldn't understand the reason I wanted to hold her so badly.

That crazy kiss comes back to me, too. How I pressed my mouth harder against hers when I should have pulled away.

And holding her hand backstage. I knew she hadn't meant to grab mine, and I could have let go, but I didn't want to. It felt right to be beside her. Which is why I ran.

Now, what am I doing?

I know that Justin wants me to avoid an improbable and dramatic situation.

The idea of never seeing Sarah again makes me feel ill.

When I watched them get on that plane I was confused and it hadn't hit me. Then realizing that Simone was bailing on the song pissed me off. But now that I'm stuck with the reality, it's Sarah I'm going to miss. Barking at her during recording was part of the fun. She could hold her own and I didn't have to sugarcoat anything. Whatever I was feeling, it was right out there and she could handle it.

Just like she could handle that bar brawl. She jumped on that guy to help me out, slapping his head and shouting at him like a wild thing. She was protective of me, which is insanity since she's so fucking tiny.

Not many women would do what she did.

What the fuck have I been doing all these months?

How did I not see her?

"Can I get you something to drink?" the flight attendant asks me.

"No. Do we have wi-fi on this flight?"

With apology in her eyes the attendant shakes her head. "We normally do, but we're having technical difficulties. Did you want something to drink?"

"Nah. Thanks."

Justin's voice interrupts my disappointment. "Take that as a sign." Off my look, he smirks. "You were going to text Sarah."

"No, I wasn't."

"Don't lie to me," he mutters, turning away. "I know you better than you know yourself. Just let it play out. You'll know what to do when the time comes."

16

SARAH

"I can't believe he hasn't called me!" Simone fumes, pacing in our apartment. She picks up a pillow and throws it across the room. "What the fuck?"

Sighing from the couch we've had since college, I ask, "Why are you so surprised?"

"Why am I surprised?" She turns to me, aghast. "Are you serious. Sarah, you know Jason is the first man to ghost me."

"You ghosted him first."

"But I always do that!"

"I know."

She screams, throwing her arms up like she's going to pull her hair out.

I'm secretly very shocked, even though I'm acting nonchalant. I really did expect him to call her after we heard from Mark that he notified Jason it's all him from here. I imagined he would at least cuss her out like he's done with me so many times. The man doesn't keep his mouth shut when he's pissed off.

My respect for him is growing, and that's doing nothing to abate the desire I have to text him. For some reason this week away from the war he and I regularly fought hasn't made me exhale with relief.

Quite the opposite.

I think I miss the battle. And I know I miss him.

"I wonder what choir he used," I mutter from deep within my thoughts.

Her voice is agitated as she shoots back, "I'd like to know, too!"

"I was looking forward to hearing the boys sing. I think it would have been so cute."

This sets Simone off and she runs to her phone. It rings in her hand and she stares at it. "That's weird."

The phone is still ringing. Is it him? My heart just skipped in a way I'm not comfortable with. "Who is it?"

"Mark," she mutters, swiping her thumb across the screen to answer. "I was just going to call you! It's so strange that you…" she trails off as he interrupts her. Her eyes go alarmingly wide and her jaw slackens. "Say that again."

"Is it good news?" I smile, sitting on my knees.

She doesn't hear me. Her face transforms to pure rage and she shouts, "What?!" Collecting herself, she stammers,

"I'm sorry I just shouted that. I'm just surprised is all. When did you find out?" As she listens, Simone locks eyes with me, stunned.

"What is it!? I can't take the suspense!"

"Oh my God…what am I gonna do, Mark?" She waits for his reply, and is clearly unhappy with it. "I guess I don't have another choice. I'm so sorry this happened. Of course, thank you for calling me. I hope you have a good day."

She hangs up and stares at me. Holding the phone in both hands she walks slowly to the window.

"Simone!" I cry out, running over to her. "What happened?"

Turning she meets my eyes with a helplessness I've never seen in her. "Jason quit the album. He didn't go see the choirs. Mark called for progress and found out that Jason is no longer interested in working with me." Her voice went up a little on those last few words.

I whisper, "Oh my God."

The phone clatters to the ground as Simone grabs my arms. "What am I gonna do?"

I'm so shocked my mouth opens but no words come out. He's dropped the whole album?

Are all the little tweaks taken care of?

Wasn't there another remix?

I'm never going to see him again?

A hollowness overcomes me while she says, "Mark said I have to find another producer. He sounded so cold, Sarah. What if they drop me, too?"

All I can do is blink.

The last time I saw Jason was really the *last* time.

As Simone rambles on with a speech about how awful this is for her career I slowly cross to the front door, unlock the deadbolt and sleepwalk out of our complex.

I'm past the lobby and outside already when she catches up with me. "Sarah, hey! What are you doing? I turned around and you were gone! I was just standing there talking to myself!"

"He's gone," I whisper.

"Yes, he's gone. I can't believe it!"

"Oh Simone," I rasp, feeling guilty and hurting at the same time.

"We have to get him back."

"No," I murmur, lowering myself to sit on a patch of grass. The sun is shining on my face but the air is so crisp it's biting my bare shoulders. Winter is coming.

She kneels down with me. "Yes! I have to prove to Mark that I'm not some artist people like Jason don't want to work with. Do you know some of the huge names he's done albums for?"

It's a rhetorical question. She knows I know, because

I'm the one who did the digging when we first heard his name. I had a feeling that rapper knew his shit and I wanted to see who this Jason Cocker guy was.

It was me who talked Simone into going to Atlanta.

And it's me who has to talk her *out* of going back.

I have feelings for Jason that are not good for my friendship with her. Something terrible has happened and this hole in my heart is the worst I've ever felt, but I'll get over it. She's my best friend. She's like my sister. And I'm crazy about the man she's just spent four months in bed with.

The man who just quit her.

The man who I want to see so badly I can hardly breathe.

"Prove to Mark that you can find a producer as good as Jason is," I choke, not recognizing my own voice.

Simone blows me off with a wave of her slender hand. "No. It has to be Jason. He's the best there is."

Voice strangled, I argue, "That's an exaggeration."

"I know you don't like the guy, personally, Sarah, but you have to admit he is an amazing producer. And it's not only that. He dumped me! I have to get him back. I have to make him pay! He's going to know dropping me is the worst mistake he's ever made!"

Where is that fucking time machine?!

"Help me," she begs.

"Oh God," I groan covering my face. "I can't."

Mistaking my denial as modesty or exhaustion or something other than heartbreak, Simone touches my arm and coaxes, "Yes you can. You can do anything. You've always been the engine, Sarah. I need you. I can't lose this record deal. Please!"

"Don't make me do this."

"Mark has to see I'm easy to work with. I am! You're the one who's the hard-ass."

I almost choke on my laughter. My brain is swimming with ideas despite my best intentions. "We could have a choir sing for him."

She sits back on her heels. "What do you mean?"

"We could go find the right choir ourselves and then have them sing an apology. Just a simple I'm sorry."

Her blonde eyebrows nearly turn into a bow. "I'm not going to beg him!"

"It's not begging. It's apologizing."

"No way."

Do I really have to persuade her to go now?

Is someone laughing at me up there?

"Simone, he quit. Your career is on the line. You have to say you're sorry or there's no way he'll work with you. That's just a fact."

"You say it for me."

"Oh my God, no! You have to say it!"

Her lips stubbornly purse and she snaps, "Fine. I'll say it but I'm not having some choir do it for me. I mean, really. That's too fucking...sweet."

"Simone, think. Put your ego aside and listen to the genius of this. *He* thought of the choir. *He* will love to hear them do this. And *you* need him, so do what will make him happy, not you! He'll probably think you're so sweet he'll want to do the other remix, too!"

Her eyes begin to light up and a smile curves upward. For the first time I don't think she looks pretty. She looks a little like the Grinch before he steals the toys in Whoville. "And that'll be the two birds with one stone thing." Off my confusion she explains, "It'll get us back together."

I don't know how I'm certain of this, but I know for a fact that those boys are going to melt Jason's heart. He might be a hard-ass but it's Justin's who is cold. Jason's temper is so hot because he feels things deeply, and anyone who does will not be able to resist the sweetness of little kids singing in harmony right there on his doorstep.

My heart sinks. "Yes. It will."

"It's Friday!"

"So?"

"We book a flight for tomorrow and then we can go to that church Sunday morning! Jason said he heard they were the best. They probably are!"

"It's going to be very expensive booking a flight with this short of notice," I mutter, dreading it.

"I don't care! I'll put it on my credit card. When this album goes live I'll be able to pay it off anyway. And I have to make Mark trust me again and not drop me from the label. I'd take out a loan if I had to! Come on! Book the flight!"

She jumps up, but I struggle to stand. Everything feels heavy as we walk back inside our building together.

Seeing Jason with her again will hurt me so badly. I know that now. But I have a responsibility to do the right thing here. Help her dream get back on track, the one we've worked so hard to make a reality.

If the side-effect is them reuniting, I'll have to take it like a champ like I always do when life serves up a sucker-punch.

It's not like I ever had a chance with a man like Jason Cocker anyway.

17

SARAH

I haven't been to Mass since I was little girl. I remember wondering why we had to sit and kneel all the time, and not much more than that.

This Mass has me near tears as eighteen boys between the ages of six and eleven sing *Ave Maria*. I grab Simone's hand and she squeezes back, equally enthralled.

Since I'm good at my job I've already gotten in touch with the coordinator, Mr. De Silva, so when the parishioners file out when it's all over, easily chatting amongst themselves and greeting familiar faces, Simone and I rise from the second wooden pew to introduce ourselves in person.

Smiling he turns from telling the boys they've done well. "Stay put for just a moment."

Instantly their well-behaved demeanor transforms into normal children as they break off into conversations amongst each other while he walks to us with his hand extended.

"Mr. De Silva, they were so beautiful!" Simone smiles, gently clasping his hand in both of hers.

"Thank you. We're very proud of them." He shakes my hand next. "Now, what you're asking us to do is out of the ordinary but I've spoken with the parents since you called yesterday."

"It was Sarah who spoke to you." Simone motions to me so I can take over.

"So nice to meet you. I was in tears. They're extraordinary."

He smiles that serene smile of the spiritually evolved. "I'm glad you think so. We're very proud of them."

He clasps his hands over his rotund stomach and explains, "They listened to some of your music, Ms. Ross-Taylor, and were impressed it wasn't the sordid kind."

Simone smiles on a faint blush, "Oh no. My songs are about love and forgiveness."

I almost gag.

She continues, "Which is why we need your help. Sarah told you that I made a mistake and angered the man who's helping produce my next album. He's very talented and I need him so much. I know it's a lot to ask but, well, what did the parents say?"

His face changes to bemused. "Well, I really didn't think they'd accept. I told them of your dilemma and found them to be unmoved."

Then why are the children still here, I'm silently wondering.

His smile grows as he leans in and says in a lowered voice, "But it turns out fame is a huge draw for people these days. When they saw that video you have up, the one with over five million views, they changed their minds."

Simone's jaw slackens on a glance to me. I can read *five million*?! in her eyes.

She turns that excitement into effusive gratitude by grabbing his hands and shaking them like crazy. "Oh, thank you! I don't know what to say! That's amazing!"

He laughs and motions behind him. "Let's teach them what you want to sing."

"Do you know that song by Brenda Lee — *I'm Sorry?*"

He nods, letting his memory wander back in time. "Isn't that a love song?"

"We're not going to sing that far. I only want to sing the first lines and then have the boys harmonize it with some ahhhs and such? How does that sound?"

His eyes flicker as he pictures it and a pleased nod turns him around. "Boys, settle." It's impressive how quickly they turn to him and drop everything they were doing. To Simone he asks, "Would you like to help?"

She squeals in happiness. I would, too, if I knew how to do what she does and had this opportunity.

We both shimmy out of the pew because with the kneeling stools still down there's very little space to walk. Then I take my usual position, standing back so she can do her thing.

"Boys, this is Simone. You remember her video?"

There's lot of nodding and adorableness. I want to put them all in my pocket and keep them! One little boy who must be no older than seven is clapping his wrists together. There's no sound. Just that cute, excited gesture.

"Hi guys," she smiles. They're clearly in awe of her. "This is what we're going to do. *I'm sorry…so sorry…that I was such a fool!*" She stops singing and smiles, "You wanna try it with me?"

They nod and slowly join in as she starts over, catching up when they remember the words. After a few more tries, all the parents applaud from the pews around me.

My smile expands as the boys grin with happiness that they're getting it now.

Simone goes through it a few more times until the boys are explained the harmonies. She demonstrates what each one should be. Mr. De Silva guides the boys, choosing the ones from his experience, who can hit each note best. It's only a half hour of our time before they have it down perfectly, and it's so beautiful I can hardly stand it.

"Thank you so much!" Simone exclaims, rushing

forward to shake their little hands. The smallest one raises both his arms up high for a hug and she melts, giving him a big one. Turning to me, she touches her chest with a *can you believe them* look.

I am just beside myself.

She shakes Mr. De Silva's hand and thanks him profusely. "We'll see you in a few hours then?"

"Yes, after lunch and nap times."

"Nap times," Simone whispers. "Oh, that's so adorable. See you soon! Thank you again."

He's beaming at her. Everyone who sees this side of my friend falls in love with her. You can't help it. She just glows.

As she and I head out she waves to the parents. "Thank you everyone!"

A few moms come over to shake her hand and tell her how much they enjoyed *Just For Me*. One says with a shy smile, "I wish I could sing like you!"

"I know the feeling," I laugh.

Simone isn't very modest usually, but this setting has an impact on her. A deep red blush works its way into her cheeks. When the bright Atlanta sun hits our faces outside, she whispers, "I can't believe that just happened." She takes my hand. "I almost didn't let you talk me into this."

I nod and give her hand a quick squeeze before letting

it go as we head down the stairs for our rental car. This time we got a Toyota. The money hasn't come in for her Porsche just yet.

"Someday soon," we said when we picked up this more practical car.

For the first time since Friday, I'm feeling like I can face what we're about to do. "You're going to have to say it's your idea."

A frown pierces her forehead and I love her for this hesitation. Especially since she's been known to claim ideas that aren't hers.

"If you're going to pull this off, it has to have come from you."

At the passenger door she looks over the car's white hood with a little sadness. "I'll always know it was you, Sarah. Thank you."

Emotion tugs inside me. I nod and bite my lip, climbing in. "I'm just glad Justin said he'd make sure Jason would be home then."

"I know!" The door clicks beside her as she slides her handbag between her feet. "Why didn't he ask the reason? Justin seems like he'd be the more suspicious type."

"I have no idea. You'd think my stalking him on Facebook would have made him grill me for the why. Who knows? He said he'll do it and that's all that matters."

"Let's eat! I'm nervous."

Smiling at her, I turn the ignition. "Most people can't eat when they're like that."

"Well, I'm not most people," she mutters.

"No, you're really not."

I know for sure, I'll be eating like a parakeet.

18

JASON

"Okay, what the fuck is going on?" I demand as Justin throws salmon into a pan filled a quarter of the way with chardonnay.

"I'm poaching fish. What does it look like?" he smirks, shaking dill weed over the two fillets.

"You've never cooked for me in your life."

His eyes are bright as he laughs, "Well then it's about time I did considering you always steal my food. This'll make you owe me."

"And that look on your face," I shout, pointing at him and feeling like a detective. "You're happy. Something's happened. Tell me!"

His laugher falls to a secretive chuckle. "Nothing to tell. But I am getting a kick out of you being so suspicious. Broccoli or roasted carrots?"

I spin my baseball hat around on my head so that it's

backwards and I can see him better because this is a fucking miracle and I don't want to miss a moment. "You're gonna roast carrots for me and there is nothing goin' on?!"

"Just wanna make sure my brother has a balanced meal."

I cross my arms and snort, Jimi Hendrix shirt pulling across my muscles. "You hate eating with me."

Turning for the fridge he produces both vegetables and mutters, "I eat with you all the time."

"And you always say you hate it."

"Because you steal my food!"

"You don't eat it fast enough!"

It's his turn to snort. "Dickhead."

"Asshole."

A grin flashes on his face as he pokes the salmon around and slips the lid back over it. "Let's watch Netflix."

"Are you trying to get in my pants?"

He laughs, "Go put something on."

"Okay, I'll play along. But whenever you get the urge to come clean about the secrets and mischief in your eyes, I'll be right over here with open ears."

"Secrets and mischief? Thank God you don't write the songs you produce."

I make a wounded noise and head for the remote. The fifty-two-inch flat screen explodes in color and sound, images of the Netflix library flashing by as I search. "So you want a romantic comedy?"

"Yes," he smirks. "Please give me a reason to punch you in the face."

"Don't touch my face. It's finally healed."

"I had a lot of explaining to do at the office," he agrees, with a smile.

"You told me. I see you every day. Come up with some new stories."

"Hey, I'm cooking for you for the first time. How much newness can your psyche take in one afternoon?"

Eying him I plop down onto the couch.

"You're not going to help me?" he asks with fake innocence.

"I'm not falling into that trap. You wouldn't let me help, fucking control freak, so don't act all hurt."

"You know me too well," he mutters under his breath, focusing on slicing broccoli florets from their thick base.

The meal ends up being delicious, which I tell him by way of a couple big-eyebrow'd grunts as we watch Zoolander for the hundredth time. Today is the first I've laughed since I got home. Hanging out with him and watching a movie we still both find funny after all these years, is enough to make me forget my suspicion of his motives.

Until there's a knock at the door.

Mid-laugh at something Ben Stiller says, I look over and notice Justin's face. His laughter died at the interruption. He's watching me with a look that says the secret is about to be revealed.

"What's on the other side of that door?"

"Go and check," he shrugs.

"Oh, you have no idea, do you?"

"Not really, no."

"That's not a whole no."

Shoving me off the couch he rises up, too. "Just go answer it."

My heartbeat picks up. For some reason I have a feeling this has something to do with Sarah. Justin's peculiar behavior has a matchmaker vibe to it, and he knows I've been depressed since I decided to follow his advice and leave this touchy situation alone.

If she's on the other side of this door, I'm going to kiss the bastard.

I glance back to Justin. He motions for me to get on with it. "Are you gonna fucking open the door or what?!" he whisper-yells.

Holy shit, I'm nervous.

Outside my warehouse loft I find Simone in the parking lot in front of me, standing centered between somewhere near twenty boys. The corners of my eyes tighten in surprise as I try to understand what is happening.

Then they start to sing.

I grab onto the doorframe as the choir perfectly supports Simone's angelic voice, all of them singing Brenda Lee's famous *I'm Sorry*. When they break into harmonies, the twinkling voices hitting every note to its highest potential, it is so beautiful goosebumps light up my chest and arms. As the voices slowly fade, Simone holds her arms out and walks to me. "Jason," she smiles, looking the most beautiful I've ever seen her. "I'm sorry. I was a fool."

Blinking, I let her wrap her arms around me. We have an audience and they're all staring at us with smiling faces. Blown away by the romantic gesture, I hug her back and over her shoulder lock eyes with Sarah. Our gaze lingers. She raises her hand and waves with an awkward smile.

Simone releases me and my arms hang to the side I'm so stunned. "Jason, let me introduce you to the boys."

Each one shakes my hand and I call Justin over to meet them. Two of the boys are twins and they get a kick out of seeing me and my brother together and all grown up.

"You're not wearing matching clothes," one says.

Chuckling, Justin says loudly enough so their mom can hear, "No, we were taught to be our own men."

She hears his message, face flushing. I throw him a look, taking the opportunity to glance to Sarah.

She's watching me, her expression unreadable.

My concentration is interrupted by parents coming to meet me, overlapping voices explaining how much they love the song and can't wait to have their sons be a part of something so fun.

I cock my head. "The song?"

"We saw it on YouTube."

"Oh right! Yeah." I glance to Simone. "It's going to be great."

Simone bounces a little, ecstatic I'm on board again, and I turn back to the parents because I've kinda been roped into something without the ability to say no.

But how could I turn down these talented kids? Music is my life. Their voices are pure magic, and this song is going to be fucking...

"Fantastic," I whisper, lost in my thoughts as the parents ask if I know when we'll be recording. "Um, let me look into my schedule and we'll find a time that works for everyone. We'll send over the lyrics right away."

"I'm Mr. De Silva, the choir's coordinator."

"He's more than that," Simone smiles. "He's their conductor!"

He has a nice, friendly face, and I offer him a grin, shaking his hand. "Nice to meet you, Mr. De Silva. You've done a great job."

"You too," he beams.

As he tells me something I can't hear because I'm so distracted by wanting to talk to Sarah, I glance to where she was standing.

She's not there anymore.

Simone touches my arm and tells him, "I'll work with the boys and help them prepare before we go to Jason's studio."

After a few more questions, the parents gather their children and everyone heads to their cars.

Simone turns, "Justin. Thank you so much for helping."

"No problem," he mutters eyeing her.

When Simone's eyelashes flutter to me, I ask, stupefied, "This was your idea?"

"Uh huh," she smiles, eyes shining. "We're going to get some food. You want to come?"

"Justin just cooked. I'm full. You guys go."

I need a moment to process what just happened. Justin helped Simone? I never saw that coming.

Her smile falters with disappointment. "Okay. Can I come by later?"

I feel like I've been punched. She's never asked to see me. It's always me doing the chasing.

"Uh…"

A seductive grin appears and she bites her lower lip. I blink at her because I normally jump like a dog doing tricks for biscuits when she looked at me like this.

That old zing is no longer here.

But she can't see that. "I'll see you later then," she smiles as if it's been decided, turning on her heel and practically skipping toward a white Toyota. In the driver's seat, faced away from me, is curly red hair.

Justin claps a hand on my shoulder. "You're fucked."

He goes inside and I follow, not wanting to get caught staring after the car.

"You knew about this?" I ask him.

"Not really. They asked me to make sure you were home."

"They?"

He's lost in thought and shakes his head. "I'm happy for you."

His frown is stubborn and leads me to believe otherwise. "You are? You don't look happy."

"I'm taking it in, Jason. Just like you. But yeah, I'm happy for you. I didn't want you dropping the album." I'm about to interrupt but he cuts me off. "It's going to be big, Jase. It's going to be fucking huge. That choir... that was brilliant on your part." He heads for the hook where he hung his keys and adds a somber, "Have fun tonight."

Frowning I mutter, "Yeah, thanks," and go for the remote to turn the paused movie off. I'm not in the mood to finish it. Neither is he.

I'm lost in thought when I hear him say, "Jason?"

I glance over. "Yeah?"

He pauses, and his eyes drop to the floor. "Nothing. I'll see ya." He disappears, the door clicking behind him.

19

JASON

It's a funky feeling when you're looking at someone you used to be addicted to, and that high is gone. Simone gliding around my loft in a new dress, she's clearly one of the most beautiful women I've ever seen. But the charge isn't there anymore. She might as well be my sister. I don't have any, but if I did, I suspect this is what it would feel like.

"Where'd you guys eat?" I ask as I reach into the fridge for some beers.

"The Vortex. Do you know it?"

Snorting, "Do I know it? Best burgers in town. Little Five Points or Midtown?"

"There are two?" she asks with big eyes. I can tell she's trying to flirt.

Casually I answer, "There are. One is connected to Laughing Skull, a comedy club. My brothers and I go there all the time."

"Really?" she asks, squishing her nose up. "It's so smoky in there. I didn't like that."

Popping the tops off a couple of bottles, their caps go flying as I argue, "Are you kidding? It's a city landmark! That menu is off the charts funny. The burgers are incredible. And they play classic rock!"

"I'm not a fan of classic rock. It's more for guys than girls," she says with a saucy smile.

"Are you crazy? Tons of women love it."

She saunters to me and takes the extended bottle. "You're getting a little heated, Jason."

"Because I can't believe what you're saying! If it were Sarah having this conversation with me, she'd bite my head off and tell me why I should enjoy being headless."

Laying her hand on my Jimi Hendrix t-shirt she smiles, "I'm not Sarah. If I were, we wouldn't be doing this." She runs her hand down my abs. My cock stays asleep as if nothing is happening.

Taking a sip, I mutter, "You hungry?" as she leans up for a kiss.

She blinks at me. "No, we just ate. At the Vortex, remember?"

"Oh, right." I take another sip and block her second try.

Cocking her head Simone backs off and walks away,

saying over her shoulder, "You're still mad at me."

I know she did that to show me her ass. Her ass is a little flat if I'm honest, but I know she doesn't believe that. Now, Sarah's ass on the other hand...

Fuck, Jason. Cut it out. That's her friend and she's here trying to seduce you. Stop thinking about Sarah and get Simone out of here.

"I'm not angry anymore."

Fluttering her eyelashes, she asks, "Then why are you being so cold?"

"I don't know," I lie, watching her slide her spaghetti strap down her shoulder.

"Let's put this past us, Jason."

Sucking on my lips I watch her slip the other one off. She turns to me so that it drops all the way and exposes her braless tits. They're hard and ready for my mouth, and any guy would shout I'm a fool not to be taking advantage of this.

I set the bottle down and stay put, my eyes narrowing in concentration. Guess I am a fool. She smiles like she knew she could get me going, and slowly walks to me.

I'm feeling nothing behind my zipper as she glides her fingertips up her stomach and touches those rock hard nipples on a smile.

Part of me is not okay with my flaccid reaction.

She's stunning and I'm limp?

No man is ever okay with that.

Simone slips her arms around my neck and lowers her eyelids in the sexiest way. Still nothing. I swear it's just out of habit that I palm her breasts, gently at first, just caresses. Then I tweak the nipples and watch her throw her head back and moan.

Fuck, I used to love the sound of that.

She comes back up and surprises me with a kiss. Out of habit our tongues touch and my eyes close. In no time I'm seeing Sarah kissing me and my dick twitches in my jeans for the first time.

At this exact moment Simone grabs my crotch and whispers against my confused lips, "Starting to get hard. I noticed you didn't have a tent, for once, but here he comes."

She kisses me while stroking my crotch, and it's working until I fucking see Sarah in the parking lot, turning away to go to the car.

I step back from Simone, stammering as my penis deflates, "I can't do this. I'm sorry. I don't want it."

Simone backs away, too, and covers herself with her arms. "You... *don't want it?*"

"I'm sorry, Simone. I shouldn't have let it go that far. Men are stupid."

"You're just going to turn me down?"

"You girls do it to us all the time."

"*Men* never do!"

I fucking hate how she emphasized the word men, like I wasn't one.

"Hey, *women* never make men feel bad when they don't want to fuck. Just like real men don't do that to you when you say no, right?! Now pull your dress back up and go."

The shock is so strong I think if she had a knife she might try and cut me. Instead she runs at me with her fist up, one arm over her naked breasts. "I hate you!"

I easily grab her wrist and hold her away from my body. "Yeah, well, I don't hate you. I'm just no longer interested in anything romantic anymore."

"Romantic," she snorts. "It was always just fucking, Jason. That's all you were to me, a fuck, and a hell of an awesome music producer. And that's it!"

Nodding while I chew on my lips, I release her wrist with a push so that she keeps her distance.

She yanks her dress straps back on, glaring at me like she wants me dead. She storms to her handbag and heads for the door. Spinning around, she shouts, "We're still working on this album, right?"

With an ironic smirk I cross my arms. "You think I'm going to let those boys and their families down?"

"I don't know. Are you?"

"If you even have to ask that, then you don't know me at all. We're still recording it."

"Fucking asshole," she mutters, swinging the door open.

"How does that make me a fucking asshole?!" I shout at her back.

"You just are one, that's how!" she yells, slamming it behind her.

Alone in my loft, I snarl, "What the hell did I see in her?"

20

SARAH

Not going to cry. Not going to cry. Not going to cry.

Why isn't this ice cream working? I've eaten two bites and can't manage to the get the third spoonful to my trembling lips.

Not going to cry, dammit!

Shooting up from the Airbnb couch I storm to the sink to throw Rocky Road down the drain for the first time in my entire life.

"This is your fault," I mutter.

To myself. Not the ice cream.

My hips are the ice cream's fault but it's not responsible for Simone being at Jason's loft right now. Alone with him. Underneath him.

That's my fault. It was my idea to have those boys sing for him. It was me who messaged Justin and asked him to help. It was me.

I am to blame for this pain.

I ask the empty room, "Why does this feel so terrible?" as if a therapist might magically appear to help me understand my psychosis. "For months she was there with him and I was alone and it was normal. I had no problems. I was my usual grouchy self. So why the hell do I feel like I'm going to puke tonight?"

As my shoulders start to shake I breathe deeply in and walk toward the bedroom, but I never make it there. Instead my head slams into a wall and I stay pressed against it, moaning.

"Go to sleep, Sarah," I rasp. "Tomorrow will come faster that way."

But I can't move.

"This is ridiculous. I've always been fine with whoever Simone called her flavor of the month. But now a very, very big part of me wants to tell Jason to run…even if he's way out of my league and I don't have a chance with him. I know how she is! She'll spit him out and then he'll come crying to me and I'll have to stroke his perfect head and pretend like I'm just his friend. I fucking hate this. God, why does this hurt so much!"

Groaning with my eyes shut, I claw at the wall and try to disappear through it.

A voice in my heart whispers, *warn Jason. Warn him!*

"Stop it. I can't warn Jason!" I groan aloud. "That's ridiculous! And wrong! And selfish as fuck! I'd be doing it for me! Because then maybe I'd be able to get out of the shadow she keeps me in on purpose so she's the only one who's shining…"

A-ha! You finally see it!

Opening my eyes in shock, I push off the wall and hold onto my head. "No…Simone doesn't keep me in the shadows…she's always very supportive of me."

When you're supportive of her.

"No," I groan. "She knows how much I'm worth."

To her. What about you as a person? How are you going to be happy if you keep putting her first?

"I work for her," I whisper. "It's my job to put her first."

She talks down to you. She did it in front of Jason after he kissed you, to make sure he knew you were beneath her.

"Shut up! Shut up! Shut up!" I shout at the top of my lungs.

"Sarah?" A bang on the door surprises me and I look over as I hear her voice muffled through it, saying, "Sarah, I forgot the key!"

"Simone?" I rush over and unlock it to discover her hair in place and makeup still perfect. "Did you come all the way back here for the key?"

"Were you yelling at someone? Do you have a guy here?"

"What? No…" I mutter, running my hand through my hair and trying to act like I wasn't just talking to myself and need to be handcuffed and taken to a hospital. "The T.V. was on and I was yelling *shut up* at the commercial. One of those stupid tampon ones that makes us look like idiots."

"Oh. I hate those." She blinks with irritation under the surface. "Well, that makes more sense. I would have been shocked if you had a guy over."

I stare at her as she storms past me and picks up my water, drinking from it like she's been in a desert. Shutting the front door I mutter, "I could have had a man over."

On a snort she rolls her eyes. "Yeah. Okay. Keep telling yourself that." She slams the glass down and announces, "You're not going to believe this! He couldn't get it up! Can you believe it? King of Ego-land — cocky Jason couldn't get his cock to work! Totally limp."

She's looking at me like she wants me to start ripping him to shreds, laughing with her over his inability to get it up. A month ago I would have laughed myself silly, because back then my attraction to him was hidden even from me. Back then I would have gloried over this revelation and begged for all the embarrassing details so I could mock him the moment I stepped in front of his overly confident face.

But it's not a month ago.

Right now I'm just stunned. "What happened?"

"Nothing," she grumbles, running a hand through her flaxen hair. "He's just an asshole, that's all."

"Did you fight?"

"Of course we fought!"

"Over impotency?" I whisper, confused.

Glaring at me, she demands, "Why aren't you joining in on this with me? You sound like you feel bad for him!"

"I don't, I just know it's hard for guys when they're not… hard."

I sound like an idiot.

She dryly mutters, "Ha ha," walking to the couch and flopping onto it, even though her flop is more graceful than most ballet dancer's pirouettes.

"What did you argue about?"

She growls, "Over him saying he wasn't interested anymore!"

My jaw loosens as my heart starts pounding. "He said that?"

"Yes!" she shouts, throwing up her hand. "Can you believe it?!"

"No one has ever told you that before."

"No shit, Sarah. You think I don't know that? God, say something helpful here. I went over there like a fool, practically begging him to fuck me and he acted like I was a friend or something. We're not friends!"

Walking to the couch I sit next to her with absolutely nothing to say for comfort because we have never been here before. Here I was thinking I needed to warn him, to protect him — and myself for when he came crying to me — and there was no need to.

He won't be crying over Simone. He did the unthinkable, and became the first man to ever reject her.

"Sarah, how do you handle this? It hurts!"

Swallowing hard, I shrug. "I never want anyone, so it doesn't usually hurt me."

"Has it ever?" she asks, eyes cutting my way with curiosity.

"Yes."

"When?"

I can't tell her *tonight, and last night, and the night before that.* Instead I just shrug, dumbfounded. "It doesn't matter when. It was just a guy who was out of my league."

She sighs and leans her head on my shoulder. We rest against the back of the couch, her with her eyes closed and me staring off.

Before I know what I'm doing, I blurt, "You don't really care about him. You just want him because he's unavailable."

She burrows into me and whispers, "I know."

Inhaling relief that she was able to be honest, a spark of hope lights up in my heart, creating a soft glow. I don't know why it's there but I feel better suddenly. Like I might have a chance.

"I'm going to get him back," she murmurs. "I'm going to make him sorry."

The spark flickers and disappears.

21

JASON

Simone is the first to walk into my studio on the day we're recording the choir. "Hello jerk."

"Jesus," I grumble, shaking my head and narrowing a bored look at her. It's been a week since I saw her last and she's still not over it. I know she doesn't give a fuck about me, so my patience is zilch. "Are you going to be like this the whole day?"

On a superior smile she says, "Yep!"

Sarah walks in lugging a cooler that's too heavy for her, large enough to diminish her already short frame. I rush forward and take it. "Here."

Surprised and blinking rapidly she looks at me. I feel a tug in my chest at the eye contact. It's powerful seeing her for the first time since New Orleans — outside of that fucking hand-wave last week. So strong in fact that I hesitate before pulling the cooler from her. I have to turn away quickly so I can get ahold of myself.

Didn't expect the reaction I just had, no matter how many times she's snuck into my thoughts.

"These for the kids?"

"Of course they are," Simone snaps. "Moron."

Gritting my teeth I face the spoiled beauty. She steps closer to fight but Sarah jumps between us, her arms out. The scent of her sweet shampoo instantly drifts into my nostrils.

"Okay, guys. We have to get to work here." Sarah's determined eyes lock onto Simone. "This is your hit, remember?"

Glaring at me Simone growls, "Yeah."

"And Jason, you're a professional. Or at least you can pretend to be one."

I stifle a smile and step back, nodding to Sarah. "Still sarcastic, I see."

"Did you think I'd change?" she smiles, her almond-brown eyes sparkling with their usual challenge.

"Didn't want you to," I admit. Sarah's smile falters. She didn't expect that coming from me.

Simone rolls her eyes, props her hands on her hips and looks toward the studio. "So, how are we doing this?"

"I've put several mics in there for the boys. We'll record you separately—"

"—No! I want to sing with them."

"That might make it more takes."

"You're the one who makes me do too many takes! Why not just use one of the first awesome times I sing it!?"

To Sarah, because I want to see that twinkle again, I mutter, "And you call me cocky?"

Intent on making her friend happy, Sarah sighs with an impatient look. "Jason, is it possible for Simone to sing with the boys?"

This day is going to be very long. Walking to my soundboard and fiddling with something that doesn't need it, I mutter, "It is. It's just not ideal."

"It's not ideal *for you,* you mean," Simone counters.

"Fine! Jesus, I liked it better when there was just one bitch riding my ass. I'll set up another mic."

Before the fight escalates, in runs a five-year-old, dark-skinned boy, his mother close behind. "Simone!" he shouts.

Her crappy attitude transforms instantly as she bends down to receive a hug, grinning from ear to ear. "Oh, yay! I missed you, Lewis!"

She's coached them all week on *Just For Me,* and the affection is real and mutual. Another two boys come in and Simone's irritation with me disappears completely in her distraction.

Sarah greets the first boy, "Hi Lewis!" and bends to hug him.

He announces with pride, "Sarah, I ate a carrot!"

Her face is glowing as she squats in front of him to be his height. "You did? That's amazing! And you didn't cry?"

Squishing his face up he announces, "I never cry. I just hate them!"

"Because you never tried them," she offers, smoothing down his shirt. Beaming at her he nods and she continues, "And now you have. What did you think? Did you like them?"

He shakes his head, blanching. "Uh uh. I still hate them!"

On a laugh, she glances up to me. Her smile falters as she realizes I've been staring at her. I can only imagine the look in my eyes, because seeing her with that boy flashed an image of her as a mother in my mind. And I liked what I saw.

Sarah holds my look a second and then stammers to Lewis, "Well...that's perfectly fine. At least you gave it a shot." Rising up, she glances to me once more as other parents and children file in, the studio growing louder by the second.

In a volume meant for only her I confess, "It's good to see you."

She frowns then mumbles back, "I don't know what to do with that."

"Jason!" Mr. De Silva interrupts, holding his hand out.

"Hi!" I shake it and greet the room. "Everyone! I'm going to set up an extra mic, move some things around in there, and then we'll get started." Lots of people nod and the greetings continue as I maneuver my way to the sound booth's door and disappear inside to make this work.

It's silent in here except for my footsteps on the thick carpet, and the swishing of cables I drag out from storage. It's giving me a chance to think about these feelings I have for Sarah.

Glancing to the glass window while I carry a mic stand to the center of the others, I see Simone easily chatting with Mr. De Silva, her hand on Sarah's shoulder. It's understandable why I went after Simone, but I wish I could take it back.

I'm a dick for wanting to get between those two women. Selfish, you could call me. You'd be right.

But what am I supposed to do? I saw something in her I've never seen before in any woman. I saw her with that boy and imagined her talking to our son. I didn't ask for that image to pop into my mind. It came from deeper and I can't ignore it.

I know now that I can't just walk away.

As I slide the microphone into its stand and check the chord to make sure the connection is secure, I glance over and meet Sarah's eyes. We hold the look before her head dips, eyelashes fluttering to the ground in thought.

That wasn't her checking to see if everything was ready. She's torn, too. I saw it.

She cares about me.

A grin spreads on my face as I do one final test of my equipment. My chest is full, my lungs light and my body awake more than it has been since the depression set in right after New Orleans.

Strolling with a carefree air, I return to tell everyone, "Okay, let's get you boys all set up." Meeting Sarah's eyes, I add, "We're ready to go."

22

SARAH

All the boys inside the soundproofed recording room are so excited to be singing in front of microphones. Their parents and Mr. De Silva are stuffed into this room with Jason and me, quietly watching so that Jason can focus.

Lifting his hand from one of the dials, he pushes the button to talk to the singers. "Great take, boys. Simone, that was perfect. How did you feel?"

She's been very professional with him since she gained an audience, so there's no hostility behind her answer, "Great. It sounded good from in here." She touches her lucky headphones and leans into the mic to ask, "Go again?"

"One more time please. But I think we got it. Hey boys?"

They're all staring at him through the glass, some nodding.

"You're doing an incredible job. One more time?"

Almost all of them shout, "Yeah!" while the shyer two just nod, smiling wildly.

Jason glances to me, his gorgeous green eyes alight with enjoyment. His finger is off the button as he says, "I think they're having fun."

Several of the parents chuckle. Jason winks at me, and turns around, pushing the button to say, "Count in, Simone."

"Four, three, two, one…"

Their little mouths open and beauty drifts out. It's enough to make your eyes water. Mr. De Silva and I share a look where I nod to him that he's done so well with these children. Jason's fingers are traveling all over his digital soundboard, his eyes shifting from the choir and Simone to the dials and levers as he slides this one and turns that.

The ethereal choral arrangements have a melancholy to them that is perfect for the song's finish. Even as she says that she just needs herself and she's doing 'this for me,' you can hear that what she really wants is someone to share her life with, just like we all do.

As the final choral notes drift toward silence, Jason pulls two levers and holds his other hand up, tapping the air as he counts the ending down.

When they all go silent, he leans back in his chair and starts clapping. All the parents join in.

I leap forward to hit the button so Simone and the

boys can hear the applause.

Jason whispers low enough so only I can hear, "You got rid of the vanilla."

Without answering Jason, I nod to my best friend and call out, "That was so beautiful! Boys, you are wonderful and I love you all!" I back away and hug myself, emotions pooling in the corner of my eyes.

Jason pushes the button to tell them, "You can come on out. That's a wrap! We got it."

Turning in his chair he meets my eyes. He noticed I didn't answer him. Mr. De Silva traps his focus, offering his hand on the wistful, "I don't know how you can tell the difference between all those nobs, son!"

Jason grins, "I don't know how you can handle a group of eighteen artists. I have trouble with one."

The older man laughs and claps a hand on Jason's arm. I watch him gripping the bicep and wish I was that hand. "Well done, Jason."

"You too, Mr. De Silva."

Simone is all smiles and laughter as she hugs the boys one at a time, and then comes out to hug the parents, too. Each is thanked from a genuine and joyous place in her heart. That's always when she's her most beautiful, and I keep waiting for Jason to stare at her like he used to do.

But he keeps watching me and not her. While he's

talking to one of the parents about how long he's been in music, where he studied, and answering other curious questions they have for him, he keeps glancing to me.

There's a secret happiness behind his eyes that I can't understand. Is he just like her? In his element and having a great time? Or is my gut instinct telling me the truth…that he's…

No way.

Oh shit…I know what it is.

He's paying me this attention to get her jealous. Or pissed off. To get back at her.

He just lifted Dylan high in the air, both of them laughing.

Oh my aching ovaries. I mean, really? The kids love him and he's so good with them.

He'd make a wonderful father…

"Sarah!" I turn to her as Simone asks, "What'd you think?"

With guilt all over me, I force a reply, "It was ridiculously beautiful, Simm. You guys were magic."

She grins and glances to Jason, the light in her blue eyes faltering. "What'd he think?"

Tightness locks my lungs up but I manage to mumble, "He's really happy with it."

She winks at me, "Good."

As the final family leaves, Jason walks to the two of us. "Job well done, ladies."

Simone's smile twitches as she glances to me. I know what she's thinking, that I had nothing to do with the success of today. I'm not going to argue with her secret thoughts. I'm not the one with all that talent.

"Thank you. It was a lot of work, but I pulled it together."

His eyes narrow slightly, realizing she took it personally that he didn't give credit where it was due. "You did well, Simone," he coldly says. "Now if you'll excuse me, I want to work on combining what we did before, with today's recording."

He turns his back to us. Simone blurts, "I can't believe your fucking attitude."

He tenses and slowly turns, cocking his head. "Simone, I'm trying to be civil."

"Civil?!" she explodes, her previous euphoria evaporated. Motioning to the crotch area of her dress, her eyebrows rise up. "Just a month ago your face was here!"

I almost laugh because it's such a strange thing for anyone to say aloud, and I have a weird sense of humor.

But Jason isn't amused. He looms over her, eyes flashing with restraint as his voice deepens. "And then you had a temper tantrum before your show and acted like a fucking baby. And danced for some fucking frat-type lowlifes like I didn't exist. So excuse me if I'm –"

"—It was one night! I acted like a brat for one night!"

"No, Simone, you acted like a brat many times. I just didn't see it until the domino effect of that concentrated, pile-of-shit evening."

I back away, but can't take my eyes off of them. No one would be able to. Two gorgeous blondes getting in each other's faces and fighting with sharp tongues and resentment to spare. Quite the show, and for very personal reasons I have to know how it ends.

"When did I act like a brat?"

"Are you kidding? Remember when I suggested the Time Travel theme? You pouted and said you wouldn't be able to be an angel with that idea." He mimics her, badly, "'I have to be an angel for my party, Jason! There are no angels in history.' I was like, what the fuck? Really? Ever read the Bible?"

"I would have had to explain it to everyone," she seethes.

"And the time the pizza guy showed up with sausage instead of pepperoni and you called him incompetent!"

"He was!"

"You don't talk to people like that," Jason growls. "Maybe someone else had handed him the wrong one. Maybe we said sausage on the phone! Maybe someone died in his life and he had an off night!"

She throws her hands on her hips, "Oh please."

"You never know." Jason points at her. "And I could name countless times when you snapped at people just because they inconvenienced you. At least your friend Sarah here was a cunt for a reason!"

My mouth drops open. "Uh, thank you?"

As if he didn't hear me, he continues, "When she's pissed it's because she's looking out for you. But she doesn't need to do that, does she? Not with how much you look out for your-fucking-self!"

Simone's lips get all tight, then she throws those daggers my way. "Oh, I see. *Sarah's* a cunt, but somehow she's perfect. You just had to hold her hand. You accidentally kissed her! And now she gets to be a cunt and I don't because somehow you've rationalized it in your twisted head? Why don't you just ask her out, Jason? Huh?"

My mouth closes abruptly and heat turns my skin dark red. It's all of my guilty wishes being spoken out loud and I want to run.

Jason glances to me, deeply frowning. He shakes his head like asking me out is the most absurd idea he's ever been offered. "Simone," he growls, "I think you're very gifted and I'm happy to finish this album for you. But the veil is off my eyes now and I see that you and I should never have dated. It was a mistake."

Oh my God. I take two steps back to avoid the impending shrapnel of the bomb he's detonated.

"A mistake?!!!" she screams, eyes wide. "Fucking me was a MISTAKE?"

"I said *dating*!" By his expression he believes that's somehow better.

But he doesn't know how women think.

He's about to learn.

I cover my eyes as she snarls, "Oh, so you'd fuck me but you wouldn't date me? You'd take my body but not buy me dinner?! Do you think I'm some sort of low-level slut you can just use and toss aside?"

"No, I never said that," he mutters. "I just meant –"

"—Do you have any idea how many men would love to be with me?"

I peek out, thinking, *no Simone. Don't go there. Just walk away.*

But she's already en route, dignity be damned.

"Jason, do you know the emails I get? The messages on social media? I have over eight-hundred-thousand followers on Twitter! And they all want me."

"Oh God, make it stop," I whisper.

Jason is sucking on his lips. "I just meant," he tries

again. "...that working together has worked out better than dating you."

"Really?" she screeches. "Because I think it's been a disaster!" She grabs her purse and motions for me to follow her.

Jason shoves his hands in his jeans pockets. I meet his eyes and without talking he conveys that he didn't mean for it to go this badly. I give him a nod that I understand and run out after her.

"Can you believe him?" she explodes as we rush to the rental car. "Dating me is a mistake? What an ungrateful, egotistical, cocky sonofabitch bastard!"

"Yeah..." I mutter, fumbling for my keys. "I hate it when people are that full of themselves."

"Right?!" She stops at the door. "I need ice cream."

23

JASON

"Fuck," I mutter, raking my hair, and tugging the baseball hat back into place.

Running out the door I scan for their car and find it pulling out of the parking lot, seconds away from joining traffic on the busy street.

I almost shout *Sarah,* but catch myself in time.

"SIMONE!"

What the fuck are you doing, Jason?

Have you lost your mind?

Apparently I have, because I yell it again as loudly as if my life depends on them hearing me.

The car stops and I run over to the passenger side.

Simone rolls down the window and I lean in to say, "I'm sorry. Come over to my loft later on."

"You're crazy if you think I'd do that!" she snaps.

"I mean both of you. A celebration of the album being

complete. Let's bury the hatchet and start over from a professional place. I'll invite Justin, my brother Jake and his wife Drew. You can invite anyone you want."

Simone's taken aback, but she's thinking about it. I glance to Sarah and see almond eyes intently watching me. She's trying to figure out what I'm doing. She's had that expression a lot today.

This is a disastrous idea.

Nothing but chaos can come of it.

I know that deep down.

But I'm not about to let Sarah vanish forever. I'm desperate. And fucked, just like Justin said.

"Come on," I urge her, with my best smile. "Let's not end things like this."

Simone mutters, "You better buy some really expensive booze."

There go her true colors again. *Sure, I'll come Jason, if you pamper me and make it worth my time.* How did I not see through that shit for four whole months. I blame my cock. It's an idiot sometimes.

"Of course," I chuckle. "What's your poison? Vodka, gin, whiskey?"

"Tequila," she shoots back with a triumphant smirk.

"Done."

"Nine o'clock!"

She wiggles her fingers at me as the car takes off.

I turn and watch it go, locking eyes with Sarah in her rearview mirror for a brief second. Her eyes looked dead. She's not looking forward to this. Which, after that fight she just witnessed, I can understand.

"Justin," I say into the phone as soon as he answers. "How do I get Sarah to realize I'm a good guy?"

"Don't ask her to betray her friend."

"Fuck! I need another answer."

"I don't know, Jason. Time?"

"I don't have time. We just finished the recording. The work is all mine now. They'll be heading back to Michigan soon. I have to do something."

He pauses and I can hear his assistant asking him something. "Later," he tells her, before coming back to me. "How much do you like this girl?"

"Enough to picture her having my children."

"You're shitting me. Jesus, are we even related?" he growls under his breath. "Fine. I'll try and come up with something."

Pushing my hat over my eyes to block the waning autumn sunlight, I break the news. "They're coming to my place tonight. I'm inviting Jake and Drew, too. To celebrate the album."

"I'll be there," he says without hesitation "I'm in. Let's

make this happen for you."

Hanging up I dial our younger brother. "Jake! Party at my place tonight to celebrate!"

He chuckles, voice deep. "What's the celebration?"

"Finished recording a number one hit today."

"You're very confident."

"When you hear it, you'll see."

"I can't come, buddy. Drew's got the flu and I'm taking care of her."

My smile vanishes. "Oh shit, Jake, I'm sorry. Tell her I hope she gets better soon. Need me to pick up anything?"

"Nah, thanks. I got it," he says easily. Then his voice changes to mock-possessiveness. "And if anyone's going to help my wife get better, it's me."

Stifling a laugh, I offer, "Okay cool, I'll get her some whiskey. And my cock. That'll clear her flu right up."

He laughs outright. "Fuckin' sicko. I'd like to see you try that. I'll cut it right off."

"Ouch! Never joke about that."

"Never joke about my wife again."

"You mean your wife and my medicinal cock?"

"Shut up, Jason," he chuckles. "You're lucky you're not here."

My voice changes so he knows this time I'm serious. "She that bad, huh?"

"Whole body aches. Been throwing up. She's pale. I hate it. But you guys have fun. I wish we could be there."

"Me too, Jake. Talk soon."

* * *

I spend hours layering the tracks together, and since there are no windows in my studio, I lose track of time. When it hits me that I haven't looked at the clock, I burst out of my seat and lock up.

Expensive tequila. She wants it, I'll get it. But this particular booze is a dangerous choice when it comes to women.

At the liquor store on the corner of Northside and Seventeenth the backdrop of Atlanta's skyline sparkles in the distance. I stop a second and take it in. I love this city. I've been to Detroit. It's not boring, that's for definite. Can I convince her to stay here a while?

"Yeah, right," I mutter. "Like she'd live anywhere Simone isn't."

Discouraged by all the obstacles, I yank the door handle and pace through lanes of liquor bottles ranging from ten dollars to two-hundred. Behind the counter are even higher priced options. So that's where I'm headed. "Two of the Asombrosos. One of both kinds you have here."

They never smile at this place, and tonight is no different. As the guy rings me up my mind wanders to the next several hours of uncertainty. I'm on a suicide mission and those bottles are the fuel. But by the rapid beating in my chest, I'm not turning back.

24

SARAH

"You keep staring out the window," Simone mutters to my back as the hour approaches nine.

On a wary shrug I tell her, "I've been ready to go. Am I supposed to watch you changing outfits?"

While slipping the spaghetti straps of a tight, red dress onto her slender shoulders, she explains away my lack of style, "Well you only ever bring a few things on these trips. I've got ten times the alternatives."

And ten times the beauty, which is the irony. She'd look amazing in anything and yet brings an entire store-worth of dresses with her everywhere. Redundant and a waste of space if you ask me.

"I'm surprised we just had the one carry on for New Orleans," I mumble, staring at the sliver of the new moon.

Catching my sarcasm, she laughs and explains while applying powder to her forehead with a thick makeup brush,

"It was only one night. Thank God Mark was kind enough to have our things shipped from Atlanta after." She pads into the bathroom to see herself in the floor-length mirror. Popping back out she asks, "What do you think? Enough to make Jason drool?"

"Yes."

"Nice enthusiasm. And you didn't even look!"

Glancing to her I sigh, "You're gorgeous. We all know it. Let's just go." I head for my purse and don't see that she's crossed her arms and is eyeing me with a peculiar expression.

"Sarah, what's up with you?"

"Nothing. I'm fine."

"If you're fine I'm refried beans."

Cocking an eyebrow her way, I smile, "Refried beans?"

On an easy grin, she shrugs, "I'm hungry. It was the first thing I thought of!"

"You're dumb."

"And you love me." She spins around and holds her arms up. "So, this is the one, yes?"

"Yes."

The dress hugs her in a way that makes her appear curvier than she is, and with her hair curled to a light wave she's stunning. And here I am in black jeans and black, loose halter. At least I've got heels on.

But does it matter what I look like?

No, it doesn't.

If Jason thinks he's going to flirt with me to make her pay, or be jealous, or beg for him, or whatever, he's going to be disappointed.

I won't be used.

I have feelings, too.

I just don't show them to anyone.

She bends for her purse and I catch a glimpse of her silky white thong.

"Um...Simone. Might not want to do that."

Her spine shoots up. "Did you see my panties?"

"I did."

A wicked grin flashes. "Then I will definitely have to drop something tonight. I am going to make Jason's cock hard for me again if it's the last thing I do!"

Thank God she doesn't wait for me to respond with enthusiasm and encouragement, because I couldn't muster it if I tried.

The only reason I want to hurry up is because I want this night to be over.

Pulling up to his warehouse loft space I park our rented Toyota and inhale courage. Simone has checked her face repeatedly during the twenty minute drive, further cementing in me the awareness that these feelings I have for Jason are downright wrong.

I have a brother. We're not close. He has...problems.

But what I always wanted was a sister. And then I met her. She's it. It's been that way since I first started following her around after she moved to Detroit when we were juniors in high school.

Why she let me I'll never know.

But something happens when you meet certain people. You find yourself making time for them even if the match seems odd on the outside. She and I hung daily after that first conversation in Social Studies where she asked me if the teacher always talked with only her bottom teeth showing. I'd confirmed, and then we whispered about where Simone had moved from and what Detroit was like whenever Mrs. Tully wasn't paying attention, which was most of the time.

After that, Simone let me idolize her and in exchange I got to be around my hero.

Her. She was my hero.

But that glow is fading. At the hundredth reapplication of her lipstick I'm side-eyeballing her with a confused expression.

When did Simone become a human being?

I'm mourning the loss.

She climbs out first as I suck in a deep breath and slip the key into my bag, throwing my legs out of the vehicle and jumping out with my eyes down.

"Sarah! Look out!" Simone screams.

I pancake myself against the car as a Chevy truck nearly takes me out. My curly hair flies up from its proximity and speed. Panting I turn around and meet her eyes over the hood. "Jesus! That was really close."

"Your head is up your ass tonight. Try not to get yourself killed. Please and thank you."

She motions for me to join her and I trudge around the car with my heart pounding so badly it's painful. I didn't need that adrenaline rush added to my anxiety.

The door opens ahead and Jason runs out, looking fucking gorgeous in a sticky white t-shirt, jeans made for his thighs and hips, and no baseball hat. His hair is mussed up the perfect amount and my breath hitches as he locks eyes with me. "I heard your name being screamed! What happened?"

"Nothing," Simone smiles, casting a warning look to me.

I get the silent message.

No arresting his attention from her tonight in any way, shape or form. Not even with a near-death experience.

"Nothing," I nod, forcing my eyes to the ground as I keep walking to my own living hell.

25

SARAH

As we walk into his loft she and I both glance around, impressed. He's strung twinkly lights everywhere, and the music is old school R&B. Simone immediately moves her hips to the beat.

Now that I'm here a memory hits me of when he asked, "Did your rock let you come out to play?"

I wish I had a protective stone like that looking out for me. I'd crawl under it and hide this one out.

His home is an open floor plan save for the divider-wall installed in the far right corner, to add some privacy for his bed. My eyes linger there a moment, wondering what color sheets he has. I hope they're navy blue.

There is something wrong with me. I need a shrink.

Justin's at the kitchen counter in his usual uniform of a well-fitting suit, though the jacket is thrown over a chair and his tie is loose and sexy. He's standing in front of two bottles of tequila that are shaped like...penises.

You've gotta be kidding me.

I laugh under my breath and shake my head as we walk over. One is silver and the other pink with a purple gem. They're extremely suggestive, and by the way Simone's mouth turns up, she approves.

She touches Jason's face as she passes him and purrs, "Perfect choice, and they look very expensive."

"The lady demanded it."

I want to vomit, but I settle for an eye-roll. Behind her back he grins briefly at me, then gives a wink that throws me.

Why did that just feel like we're in on a private joke together? I'm not okay with making fun of my best friend behind her back, and certainly not with her ex-ish.

It's always she and I who laugh at the guys.

I like it that way.

So why did my heart skip a little?

Gritting my teeth I head for Justin, too, only now I'm walking faster. I can feel Jason's body heat behind me and he's not even that close.

I glance over my shoulder with lowered eyelashes, not wanting to look obvious.

He's locked on me so I quickly turn face-front.

Don't fall for his game.

Don't be the pawn.

Keep your eyes on anything but him.

Justin rakes an appreciative gaze down Simone's dress. "You look gorgeous. No…you look delicious."

She eyes him. "Okay, tell me what you want."

"You couldn't handle what I want."

Her head cocks. "I meant what are you trying to get from me, with the compliment."

"I know what you meant," Justin smirks, unwrapping the plastic protective seal on the pink bottle. "Calm down. I'm just saying hello." He glances to me, nodding briefly. "Sarah."

I snort.

His blonde eyebrows jump.

Couldn't help myself - the contrast of his reaction

from her to me was comical different.

"Gee, thanks Justin."

"What? I said hello."

"Okay fine," I chuckle.

Jason crosses to reach inside a cupboard, the white cotton shirt pulling at his shoulder blades, his bicep rippling. I glance to the counter because my lower abdomen just clenched.

He turns and sets small, elegant glasses down, explaining, "Asombroso Silver and Reposado. The Reposado is better so we'll begin with that."

Justin adds with a sly smile, "While our taste buds can tell the difference."

Simone leans against the counter, fingertips tracing the bottle he's about to pour from. "I'm hungry," she almost moans.

Boy, is she laying it on thick.

Jason's body brushes mine as he comes to grab tortilla chips for her out of a high cupboard. The side of my arm and hip lights up like he just ran a sparkler up them. I exit heading for the stereo to hide.

No one is talking. Just that sexy music filling the air. I'm crawling out of my skin. Fighting to keep my voice even, I call over my shoulder, "I love that you have vinyl albums."

"I've got over a thousand," Jason says, ripping the bag

of chips open and pouring them all into a large, royal blue ceramic bowl. A stray falls onto the counter and he pops it in his mouth.

"I had over fifty," I smile, lifting up a weathered copy of Duran Duran's *Rio*. "This was my first. I found it at an old record store. But then Simone made me…" I trail off as I catch her warning look.

Glancing to the shelf I slide the record back in place.

Jason doesn't want to drop it. "Simone made you what?" he asks, producing a jug of salsa from his fridge.

The picture of total relaxation, she answers for me, cutting in with, "—Donate the albums to charity." Off his look, she adds with complete seriousness, "A homeless shelter needed music. It was so — what's the word? — *dreary* there. You know how they are."

Justin makes a small noise, hiding a snort of his own. He doesn't believe her, and despite her cool delivery Jason also appears unconvinced. But he nods, unwilling to delve deeper into the bullshit she just offered him up to eat.

"Well, that was very nice of you, Simone," he says with a forced smile.

She leans toward him, "I was happy we could help."

Jason licks his lips like he's biting back a retort while loudly unwrapping plastic from the fresh salsa's lid.

His brother waves a glass in the air, beckoning me on a

smirk, "Come back to us, Sarah. You're too far away."

I walk to it, locking eyes with the devilish half of the twins.

"Thanks," I mutter, cocking my head as he holds my look.

What's up with his conspiratorial vibe?

Is it just in my head?

He hands two glasses off to Jason and Simone, who by anyone's standards are so good-looking together they could be painted on the side of a wall in Florence, Italy. I am very delusional to have feelings for that man, on many counts.

Justin holds up his glass and announces, "To *Just For Me* hitting Number One."

We all smack glasses together and I wince as some of my tequila splashes onto my hand. Licking it, I look up with a face that says *I hate being so clumsy*. But Jason's locked on my tongue licking the liquid off my dampened wrist. A jolt of arousal slams into me. I saw desire in his eyes.

"To Number One," I mutter, and we all drink.

"Let's do another!" Simone purrs, glancing between the twins. Jason pulls his focus from where it was locked on my shocked gaze and smiles at Simone.

"Count me in," he rasps.

Oh shit. What is going on?

Something is happening tonight and only two people

know what it is. The Cocker Brothers.

My muscles tense as I hold my glass out. "Pour."

Simone whoops and grins, "Uh oh, Sarah might get on a table again!"

I shoot her a look. "Never again."

"Maybe!" she smiles, holding out her glass for more liquor.

"This tastes very good. Nice choice," I say loudly, changing the subject.

After the second shot Justin begins passionately detailing the reasons why there are so many potholes in Atlanta. At five-two I'm the tiniest of anyone here, so when he absently goes to pour me a third, I wave my hand and argue, "Not yet."

He pauses to consider my refusal, grabs my glass from my hand and ignores me while he pours again and continues, "But here's the problem, the cost. It will cost taxpayers too much money and so what do they do? They keep voting against any of the bills we offer! But then they go back to griping. Earlier this year –"

Simone, bored as hell, interrupts him, "Can we change the music?"

"Justin, that's too much!" I'm pointing to the glass he's handing me. It's full.

He got too distracted. Justin is aiming for the Senate.

183

I'll be surprised if he doesn't get there, with how much he seems to love every aspect of it. I've never seen someone so fired up over holes in the ground.

As Jason goes to change the song, Justin coldly tells Simone, "You interrupted me while I was talking."

"Well, the beat behind your riveting tale was distracting me."

His eyes flicker and he decides to let it go.

From behind my tequila glass I'm secretly spying on Jason. The muscles rippling on his back as he pulls vinyl records out from multiple shelves, repeatedly bending at the knees then straightening again, are killing me. The way those jeans pull over his thigh muscles makes me feel toasty.

"You're giving up on Pandora?" I call over.

"Yep," he smiles over his broad shoulder. "I'm taking back control."

Hearing the word 'control' from his lips when I've had this much tequila has the unfortunate consequence of making me extremely moist. Shifting my weight, I bite my lip while Justin's deep voice blurs.

The more time here stretches, the more I want to stretch my legs. Wide open. And there's no one to do it with.

Fuck it.

Down the hatch.

26

SARAH

Wow, that's some good stuff right there.

"Burn baby burn," I whisper.

Simone is crunching away on chips and salsa and she's begun to tell Justin about the time we went to San Diego for her to play a club. "My band drove all the way over there with us. It was so fun. And oh my God," she breathes, staring off into the memory. "The beach at midnight! Have you ever been?"

"No." He's smiling from behind his glass, studying her as she sways with the invisible breeze. "But I'm guessing there were palm trees."

"So many palm trees! And the sand was cool on my toes. Wasn't it, Sarah?"

I blink away from Jason to her. "Yep. It was cool."

"Sooooo cool. And the night air was warm. Not like here where it's humid, but just this beautiful light wind blowing all over our bodies." She slides her hands down her breasts as if she's alone. And she's not meaning to do that – she's just getting really lubed up like I am.

We are in trouble.

Otis Redding's *These Arms of Mine* comes on and Simone moans in happiness.

Equally a fan, I start laughing with my own brand of much quieter joy. Just a tiny, under my breath laugh.

Justin reaches over and takes the glass from my hand. He sets it on the counter and starts to dance with me. His warm hand slides around my lower back while his other cups mine, old school-style. Surprised but secretly happy to be swept away, I look into Justin's eyes, my chin tilted way up.

He whispers, "Hey Sarah," to me in a voice I've never heard this devil use before. It's very sexy.

In a more hushed tone that no one can hear over the music, I whisper, "What are you doing, Justin?"

He glances over to his twin. I follow his lingering gaze and see Jason approached by Simone. But his eyes are on me and they are narrowed with fury. I've seen him pissed off before, and at my doing, so I know his rage when I see it.

Simone comes up behind him and slides her arms around his torso. He flickers and turns to take her to where Justin and I are dancing.

Frowning back up to the devilish half of this pair I see

a glint of triumph in Justin's eyes as he fixates on me. He's got something up his sleeve, but what I don't know.

Then it occurs to me for the first time…he's going to make a move!

And Jason knows Justin will use me up and toss me aside…so he's feeling protective.

That's why Jason was angry.

He knows his twin is a bad guy.

I have to get out of these arms.

But Otis isn't making it easy.

I challenge Justin with a hushed, "I'm not falling for this crap, just so we're clear."

He smirks and whirls me far enough away that Jason and Simone can't hear us. I glance over to them and see she's whispering in Jason's ear. From the look on his face, she said something very hot and dirty. Pain twists my gut.

Justin cups my chin and brings my attention back to him. "What crap, Sarah?"

Swallowing against the sadness I'm feeling at being in the wrong twin's embrace, I whisper, "I'm not interested."

"In what? My brother? Because that would surprise me very much."

My eyes widen with surprise and as Justin's hands slides lower to rest on the top of my tailbone. "Why are you fondling me if you think I like your brother?"

My eyelids go heavy under the heat of his breath as he leans down to whisper against my sensitive earlobe, "That's a really good question. Now why do you think I'm doing it?"

He hovers there, tightening his grip on my body and pressing into me. He's not hard, so what the hell is he doing?

Suddenly he's yanked off of me and there stands Jason like he's about to punch his twin in the face. "May I cut in?"

My lips part and I glance to Simone who is so shocked her mouth could hold a whole Granny Smith apple.

"Of course," Justin murmurs with a smile of pure satisfaction. He heads for Simone. "May I?"

She is speechless, totally flabbergasted and a little drunk, so she nods, holding up her arms for him to come in.

I'm scared to look at Jason. I know Simone is going to explode any minute when her intoxicated mind clicks into what just happened.

My head turns and I lock eyes with the object of my desire. His face is tight, his gorgeous eyes, darker than I've ever seen them.

He steps close and my breath hitches as he whispers his hands down and around my shaking sides until his thick fingers press into the small of my back. I shiver as he pulls me against his body. We slow dance in silence, and I feel like I might faint. I'm so terrified of the imminent explosion, but I don't want to push him away.

"Jason," I whisper, voice trembling.

"Shhh," he rasps in the shell of my ear. "She's about to blow. Just give me this one moment to enjoy."

To enjoy?

What does he mean?

Oh my god.

He's basking in the fun of making her jealous.

Agony rips into me as I shove him away. "Enough!" I shout. "God, just stop! It's cruel! Stop!"

Turns out Simone isn't the one to lose it.

Jason stares at me, speechless, eyes flitting in confusion. Or more likely embarrassment. Justin and Simone stop moving, too.

Three sets of gorgeous eyes rest on mediocre little me.

"I'm not a fucking pawn in your games!" I shakily tell Jason before locking eyes with his twin to direct my accusation at him, too. "You can stop using me to make Simone jealous. I have a heart! I have feelings! Although I'm sure you wouldn't think a bitchy little shrimp like me could have them. But I do!"

Jason's eyes narrow.

Simone struts over to stand up for me, but I see the relief barely hidden behind her protective expression. She couldn't understand how she'd been abandoned just now, and it finally all makes sense.

"That's really not nice, Jason," she says with firm annoyance.

I'm far more than annoyed.

I'm absolutely crushed.

Jason is about to say something but Justin interrupts him with, "There's someone at the door, Jase."

We all look. Over the music and my explosion, most of us didn't hear the light, slow tapping. But there it is again. Jason holds my look as he passes me to answer.

He opens the door and a very thin blonde woman falls inside. "Jason," she hoarsely whispers."

"No fucking way," his brother growls. Simone and I turn to him and he is seething. "Bernie. His ex."

Our heads whip back to see Jason tenderly picking the woman up. "There now. I've got you," he rasps to her, voice filled with pain.

Her eyelids are heavy. She looks used up, but she was very beautiful at one time. She's high and there are track marks on her arms with blood dripping down them.

"You've gotta be kidding me," Justin mutters.

Cradling the limp woman he kicks the door shut with his foot, his eyes meeting mine. He blinks to his brother, "Run some hot water. And get my First Aid kit."

Justin turns on his heel for the kitchen, mumbling cuss words under his breath that I've never heard of.

27

JASON

"Hey," I whisper to Bernie, gently laying her on my bed.

Simone stays back and stares, but Sarah hurries over to pull back the covers.

"She's trembling."

"I know," I rasp, torn up inside. Smoothing sweat-matted hair from Bernie's forehead I lean down to meet her drifting eyes.

"Help me," she breathes, unable to focus.

Justin walks over with angry strides, holding out the blue bowl. I glance to it and he reads my mind. "Yes, I washed it." He hands me a rag and I take them both, dipping the soft cloth into lightly steaming water. My kitchen sink gets really hot, which I normally hate. You have to be careful not to burn yourself. But now I'm grateful for it. He takes the bowl from my hand. I squeeze some excess water from the cloth into it and turn to wipe Bernie's pale face.

"Call 911," Simone mutters.

"Not yet. She's already been to jail once for this. Let me just…" I trail off, washing the face of the woman I once loved. Next I wash her right arm and nearly start crying. I have to turn my face.

Simone grumbles, "This is fucking ridiculous. Who is she?"

I snap, "Keep your voice down."

She storms off. I hear Justin follow her. Good, let him explain. I can't deal with her bullshit right now.

Sweeping the blood away with slow, gentle strokes, I stare at Bernadette Lancaster.

She used to just do coke.

Now heroin?

Fuck, I hate the spiral of addiction. That it's inevitable until they hit rock bottom, and everyone's is different.

When's she going to hit hers?

When's it going to end?

Sarah kneels at the side of my bed, gazing at Bernie with sadness and compassion. She must have taken the bowl from Justin because it's in her hands now, and she holds it for me. I keep my eyes averted and mutter, "Thank you."

"It's no problem."

Wringing out the cloth again, I nod and Sarah sets it

on the floor while I clean the other wrecked arm.

Sarah whispers, "Can you hear us?"

"Her name's Bernie," I choke.

She glances to me and nods, turning back to my ex and touching her cheek. "Bernie, can you hear us?"

Bernie moans. Sarah feels her forehead and then touches two fingers to her throat, checking her pulse like it's not the first time she's done this. After a good minute she meets my eyes. "She's high but she's not overdosing. Her heartbeat is strong. We have to check this jacket for drugs to make sure she can't add more to the mix."

Careful of stabbing myself with a hidden needle, I check all of Bernie's pockets and shake my head. "The stuff probably belonged to a john."

Sarah's auburn eyebrows knit together, but then comprehension waves over her as she realizes I'm saying Bernie hooks. I'm grateful there's no judgment on her face as she turns back and whispers, "Do you remember your name?"

"Bernadette," comes the moaning answer. "Bernie…"

"Good. That's very good. And you found your way to Jason's. You're safe now, Bernie," Sarah whispers. "Jason is here with you. I'm a friend of his and you're safe with me, too. Jason's going to get you out of this dress, okay?"

Bernie's blinks twice. Sarah rises to give us privacy. She

touches my shoulder on her way out. "The clothes reek of heroine. Wash her off and put her in your sweats. Want me to get them?"

Grateful and calmed by her help, I motion to my dresser with my chin. "Go for it."

My gaze dances between Bernie and Sarah as she pulls her curly hair up and ties it into a knot on the top of her head — time to work. She shuffles through my drawers and pulls out my softest t-shirt after feeling all the others. Same with the sweatpants. Turning back to me she meets my eyes.

"You have someone…?" I ask her, because she's way too knowledgeable about what to do.

Her lips purse and she gives a little nod. "My brother."

I watch her place the clothes by me. She touches my shoulder again and I cover her hand with mine for a moment. "Thank you."

She nods and slips her hand away to join the others. Bernadette's body is skinnier than I've ever seen it. She allows me to change her without a fight. Not that I'd expect one after all we've been through.

She's dead weight as I lift her arms from her jacket and hold her off the bed to fully remove it. Her dress, shoes, bra and panties all come off with equal care on my part.

She murmurs, "Thank you," several times with a voice so blurry I can hardly hear her.

But it's enough to tell me that Sarah's right.

She's not overdosing.

She'll come around.

But it's going to be a nightmare withdrawal.

She used to happily sing that fucking Amy Winehouse song to my face as if it were her mantra. "They try to make me go to rehab. I say no, no, no."

And look what happened to Amy Winehouse…joined the Twenty-Seven Club, the roster of musicians who've all died at that exact age.

Hendrix. Joplin. Morrison. Cobain.

Fucking waste of amazing talent.

Bernie's in her thirties, the same age as Drew.

They went to school together.

Wait…I should call Drew.

Oh shit, she's got the flu.

I can't burden her with this.

Especially after how much Jake hates Bernie for what she did to them and that dangerous situation she put Drew in.

No, she came to me. I'll handle this on my own.

With her tucked in, I pick up her clothes and carry them out to join the others. The conversation has been sparse from what I've heard. The music was turned off a while ago.

Simone's not happy. Her eyebrows arch up. "Like blondes, I see."

"Simone, not now."

Rolling her eyes she gets up. "C'mon Sarah."

I can tell she doesn't want to leave.

Justin stands. "Sarah can't drive. I'll take you home."

Simone glances to him, then to me. "Fine. Goodbye Jason."

I jerk my chin in response, and turn to get a plastic bag to put these rank clothes in.

My brother says, "Sarah, you should stay."

"What?" Simone snaps.

"She has experience with this." To Sarah he explains, "I overheard what you said to Jason. About your brother. Can you stay here with him to help?"

Simone's eyes lower. "I forgot about Nathan. You should stay."

Sarah glances to me. "Do you want me to?"

"Yes," I rasp on an exhale. "Please stay."

Simone waves without emotion and heads for her bag while Justin gathers his suit jacket.

He winks at me and I just shake my head.

"You three have fun now," he smirks on his way out. "Sarah." He tips an invisible hat and vanishes.

28

JASON

Now that we're alone, I don't know what to say to her. This situation is crazy, and I haven't forgotten her explosion and how hurt she was.

And how wrong.

"Your brother?"

She nods, eyelashes lowering slightly. "He's sober now. But he was a heroine addict."

"I'm sorry."

On a shrug, she mumbles, "No one's life is perfect."

"Mine is."

She meets my eyes, chuckling at my joke. "No, yours just looks perfect. Turns out you've got problems like everyone else."

There's an incredibly strong chemistry between me and Sarah that's grounded in reality. Not in some kind of idea or fantasy. It's not in my head, more in my bones. And it's

197

making it very hard not to pull her to me and explain what really happened with that dance.

Shoving my hands in my pockets I restrain myself. "You know what, Sarah, you're a walking dichotomy."

"How's that?"

"You busted my balls for months and yet in there with Bernie you were soft and kind. I like that side of you."

"Well, don't get used to it," she shoots back with a smirk. But then her face immediately softens with her voice. "What, did you think I would pull a 'drill sergeant' on her? She's sick."

"Yeah, but I saw it in New Orleans, too."

"What did you see?" Sarah whispers, looking a little scared.

"When you were dancing on that table."

Her eyes close in embarrassment. "Can we please never bring that up again?"

"You were miserable. But acting like you could hack it. And your dancing was terrible."

She laughs, "Thanks a lot!"

Her smile brings out my own. "You're welcome."

She shakes her head and walks to the kitchen. "Can I have some water?"

"Of course."

I watch her open the fridge, her curvy body perfectly

displayed in those black jeans and halter, except she's got a sports bra on. I know for a fact her breasts hang heavier than that. She's being modest.

And even in her heels she's not more than five-five. I have the strongest urge to come up behind her and pull that makeshift bun down after kissing the back of her neck, and I have to clench my jaw against the urge and keep my hands in my pockets. "You were trying to be someone you're not."

Her wall comes down then and she turns to me. "Jason, are you playing with me?"

"Playing?" I ask, tilting my head. "Oh, that's right. You were shouting earlier that I was using you to make Simone jealous."

Her eyes sharpen. "Weren't you?" She starts undoing her bun and shaking out her curls like it's a defense mechanism to have her hair back to normal. "I'm hard, I know that. I make people's lives hell when they get in the way of what's best for Simone. And I know I made yours miserable. But I don't deserve to be used. No matter what you might think."

That's it. Pulling my hands out I walk quickly to her and cup her soft chin roughly in my hand. "Hey, I wasn't using you. I was jealous. And the way he was whispering in your ear and making your eyes do that thing they're doing. I was so jealous I was about to kick the shit out of him."

199

"It's not possible," she moans.

"Why the fuck not? You're adorable. I can't stop thinking about you. It drove me nuts to see him holding you like that. It wasn't an act to get *her* jealous. I was the one who felt that way. I was furious!" Her breath hitches as she searches my eyes. "I don't use women, Sarah. That's not the kind of guy I am."

She's panting softly like she wants to run or kiss me and she can't decide which.

Her voice is hoarse as she whispers, "You're the kind of guy who makes a move on his ex's friend."

Our eyes linger on each other during my weighty pause. Slipping my hand into her soft, auburn curls, I murmur, "I'm trying to think how I can answer that and not sound like an asshole. So here's the truth. You ready?" She nods, blinking rapidly. I tighten my hold on her hair, tilting her head back a little as I bend over her. My voice is deeper now that I'm this close to her. I'm rock hard and I want to press into her. "Simone doesn't care about me. No more than I care about her. She's just pissed I called it off first. No, don't make that face. You know I'm right. You know her. She was going to kick me to the curb."

"Why do you think that," Sarah whispers, staring at my lips. It's so hot having her look at me like that, with almond eyes peering up from hooded lids. She seems so innocent, as though this is the first time a man has touched her like this. The first time a man has looked at her with longing. I can practically taste how wet she must be. I'm straining against my jeans zipper. And she just licked her lips while staring at mine.

Fucking hell.

I need her.

I need to taste her.

Struggling to keep cool, I groan, "You going to look me in the face like this and lie and tell me she wasn't gonna drop me the second she was done?"

"I can't say that."

"Can't or won't?"

Her eyes close briefly and then open in the sexiest way. "Won't."

"Fuck," I growl, "I have to do this." I press my lips into hers and feel her rise up, responding and arching her back. Unlocking her jaw with my own I seek out her tongue. "Relax," I rasp into her. She nods a little and tips her head back. Before I know it we're kissing roughly, tongues dancing with a hunger I've never felt. All I can see and feel is white hot heat.

Sarah, who always busts my balls has slipped soft arms around me, cradling my head as she kisses me, returning every ounce of passion I give her.

I jam her tiny frame against the refrigerator, gripping her lower back with one hand, her head with the other, my fingers tangled in her curls. I groan into her open lips and grind against her crotch, desperate for relief.

She moans into my mouth, whimpers, then shoves me away from her.

I back off, running my hands through my hair to gain control of myself.

I'm panting.

Harder than I've ever been.

And all I can think about is how badly I want to taste her pussy and make her scream.

"That was amazing," I rasp, locking eyes with her. "Why did that feel so good?"

"I don't know, but I can't!" she moans, sliding her hands down her stomach and clawing at her closed zipper like she wants nothing more than to rip it open.

"Do it," I moan, panting.

Turning away from me she tries to burrow into the unforgiving refrigerator door. "Oh God!"

I come up behind her and move her hair to the side, kissing the back of her neck like I fantasized doing. She presses her ass into my crotch and my eyes roll fucking back into my head. I slip both hands around the front of her jeans and cup her pussy through them. She moans and rubs on my hand and I swear I'm going to blow just from this.

My cock is pulsing for her.

Throbbing painfully.

"Sarah," I groan, tracing her earlobe with my tongue.

She moans, "I can't. Please stop." She bucks me backward and moves away from me, holding out her hand as she begs me, "Please. Stay over there."

Out of breath and licking my lips like she's a piece of steak I growl, "I've gotta fuck you!"

"Jason," Bernie's voice interrupts us.

Sarah and I fall into total shock. Shame waves over her eyes and I'm just speechless. "Go," she whispers, her voice hoarse and face stricken.

Adjusting myself and feeling shame flash into my blood, I groan, "I can't believe I forgot."

Sarah covers her mouth, shaking her head that she can't believe we both lost ourselves that much.

I walk to the divider, rushing to Bernie, and gasp when I see her.

She's unconscious.

"SARAH!" She comes running. "Check her pulse!"

Two shaking fingers go to Bernie's exposed neck. Sarah counts and then looks at me, waiting for enough time to pass. She closes her eyes a moment and whispers, "She's asleep. Her heartbeat is almost normal now."

"Thank God," I croak.

Sarah smoothes Bernie's hair and murmurs to her that she's going to be okay. She slides onto the floor with her back resting on the side of the bed. I'm sitting on it with Bernie's hand in mine. We stay here like this for a long time.

Finally I see Sarah's lips go lax as sleep starts to pull at her. She closes her eyes and rests her head, legs all twisted into a pretzel, arms hugging them.

She's a good woman. She's grounded, and when needed, she's kind.

"Sarah," I whisper.

Her sleepy eyelids flutter halfway open. "She okay?"

"C'mere." Bending, I lift her off the hard floor. She slides her arms around my neck and gazes up at me before her eyes flit quickly toward Bernie. "Don't worry. She's safe. She was snoring a minute ago. It's time for you to get some sleep, too."

29

JASON

A quick frown pierces her eyebrows, but she doesn't argue. Instead she lays her head on the nook of my chest and shoulder while I hold her tight and carry her to my couch.

That same sensation I felt at that bar comes over me, a strong need to protect her from the world. Evolution hasn't knocked that out of men yet, I guess, because carrying my tiny former-nemesis makes me feel greater than my normal self. Like all she needs to get through life is me.

"Here," I murmur, laying her on the couch and pulling down my throw blanket to slide over her body. "I'll get you a better blanket. Wait here."

"Can I have some water?" she whispers, near sleep.

"Demanding bitch," I mutter.

With her eyes closed, she smiles. "Ass face."

I chuckle and head to the fridge, grabbing a glass and pouring from my Britta pitcher. Then I go to where my towels, sheets and blankets are kept, and feel around until I find the softest one.

Tucking it around her I glance to her face and find her watching me through hooded eyes. She smiles, "Be careful, Jason."

"Why's that?"

"If anyone saw this they'd think you were a nice guy."

A grin flashes on my face, but I force it back to argue, "It's all an act. I don't care at all about you."

Her eyes flicker, her smile ghostly. "Don't you?"

Tingles travel down my torso. I run my fingers up her side, over the blanket, and meet her eyes. "I do, actually."

After a moment, she whispers, "Why?"

"I love pain?"

She laughs and rolls over so I can't see her face.

Unwilling to let that happen, I climb on top of her and push my way against the back of the couch, now inches from her face. "Nice try. You can't hide."

A playful grin tugs at her pink lips, but she's fighting it. "I can run though."

Becoming serious, I rasp, "Please don't."

Her smile fades and she reaches up and touches my face. I turn my head and kiss her fingertips, beginning to climb on top of her. She stops me. "No."

Hesitating, I lower my forehead onto her collarbone.

"I can't do this to Simone."

"Talk to her then." I lift my head. "But don't leave Atlanta yet."

Sarah's eyes go wide. Searching me, she whispers, "You're serious."

"I am. We have something here."

A sound of disbelief escapes her. "This isn't just the tequila?"

I'm stunned for a second, and then I start cracking up. "No! It's not the fucking tequila." I kiss her once and pull up to say, "I mean it. Stay."

"I have to work…"

"No, you're scared she'll be angry."

With fear in her eyes, Sarah nods a little.

"Do something for yourself, for once."

"She's a part of me, Jason."

Justin's words come back to me, how he said their connection was strong like his and mine. "Okay, it's just a little time. Can you give me time?"

"For what?"

"You want me to say it?"

"Yes."

"I need time to make you fall in love…with this city."

Sarah stares at me. "Let me talk to her."

"That's all I'm asking for."

Sarah frowns and I kiss her nose and then her lips. She responds at first, but I can feel the tension in her now. I pull back and climb off her. "I'm going to check on Bernie."

"Okay. Want me to come?"

"No. I carried you here for a reason. Rest."

She smiles as I walk away, feeling like a teenager who just asked the prettiest girl to go out with me. And she has to think about it. Sarah might not be a model or a superstar, but to me she's becoming far greater than both.

Bernie is sleeping it off. I take her phone and keys and hide them so she can't escape. Then I grab a sleeping bag from my storage room, lifting it on my shoulder as I head back to the couch. Sarah's eyes open slightly as I move the coffee table so I have room.

"You're sleeping on the floor?" she groggily whispers.

"If I sleep on the couch with you my dick will be hard all night."

"God!" she chuckles. "At least he's honest!"

Grinning, I unravel the bag and climb in it, muttering, "There is that."

She rolls to face me and hangs her arm over the side. I take her hand and lay it on my chest, eyes locked with hers. "Goodnight, Jason."

"Cunt."

Her eyes sparkle. "Penis on legs."

Laughing I shut my eyes. "Ain't that the truth...night, Sarah." I give her hand a squeeze and let my mind drift off to sleep.

30

SARAH

I wake up before Jason and watch him sleeping on the floor, his mouth open and one arm above his head, the other over his stomach. His gentle breathing continues as I stare in wonder while trying to believe he meant those things he said. He seemed sincere and I feel light inside, like maybe God's smiling at me for once.

I know I have to talk to Simone. I'm hoping she'll be able to confess again that he doesn't mean anything to her other than someone she needs for her music. And maybe she'll give me her blessing and let me stay here for a week or so. Just to be with him.

Be with Jason.

What a wild thought.

Groans from his bed in the far corner of the loft make me rise up, carefully slipping off the couch to check on Bernie. "Jason," I hear her moan before I'm around the divider. As I come into view she frowns in confusion. "Who're you?" She's clawing at her legs, and one is twitching. No, both are. I've seen this before in my brother.

"I'm Sarah. I was here last night with some other friends, when you arrived. Are you in pain?"

"Fucking hurts. Where's my purse?"

"Jason put it somewhere. But there weren't any more drugs in it anyway." Off her look I sit on the bed, my hands clasped over my lap. "I know that's what you want."

She attempts getting up and hisses, "You know nothing about me."

"My brother is an addict."

She looks at me like an animal cornered in a cage, wondering if it can trust the person with the key.

"I've been with him when he was in withdrawals, like what you're going through now." Gritting her teeth, she waits for me to continue. Or maybe she has nothing to say. So I go on, "He's clean now. He has a small store in Detroit, where I live. Sells comic books. Graphic novels. Toys. Things he loves. He's doing well. Been clean for years."

"Good for him," she mutters, pushing at her legs and rolling on her side.

But I know I saw a spark behind her eyes. "Jealousy's a map."

"What?!" she growls.

"I saw the look you just had. It was jealousy. And you know…it's a map," I repeat.

"What are you talking about?"

"Jealousy shows us what we want. When I said my brother has his life back, and is doing something he loves, you got jealous."

"I was *angry* that you're talking to me!"

With patience disguising my compassion I shake my head and hold her eyes. She was once beautiful. It's hard to see with her skin so gaunt and her hair thin like it is now, but the ghost of what she once looked like is evident in her bone structure, and you can just tell she was gorgeous.

"Anger is a mask that covers other emotions. Hurt. Pain. Jealousy. You can have your life back just like he does. Wanna know how I know that?" She just stares at me, but she's still listening, so I continue, "Because we all gave up on Nathan. He overdosed four times, but didn't die. God didn't give up on him like we did. And deep in my brother's heart, Nathan didn't give up on himself. Even when he stole to get the heroine, beat people up, and took money from a church, he still believed that he could be better than that. That he could have a life. That he wouldn't have to be in pain all the time. And so one day after writing with his own blood on a wall, *God, don't leave me,* he passed out. The owner of the hotel found him. And you know what was crazy? The owner's sister was an addict, so he didn't judge my brother or turn his back. Instead he knew exactly where to take him, the same place his sister had gone five years before to get her children back. And she'd stayed sober, so the owner thought Nathan might have a chance, too."

Tears are in Bernie's eyes. Shaking her head, she chokes, "I'm afraid."

"Of what?"

"Of failing."

I reach over and take her hand. "We're all afraid of that. But aren't you failing now? Wouldn't it be better to try a different way? Maybe if you do, and you fail a couple times at getting sober, then one day you'll succeed? Or hell, maybe you'll succeed the first try? Crazier things have happened."

Pain contorts her face and she grips my hand so hard it hurts, but I don't let go.

Jason steps around the divider, his hands in his pockets of the jeans he slept in. His pale green eyes glance from me to Bernie. She starts to weep and he goes to her. I stand and back up to give them space as he takes her in his arms. "Jason, I want to try to get clean," she says through wracking sobs. "I can't do this anymore. I was so scared last night. He made me do the needles. I never wanted to do needles! They're so awful and I couldn't say no. I tried but I couldn't!"

"Shhh…it's okay. He's gone now. He's gone. I'm here. You're safe."

31

SARAH

"Simone?" I call out, quietly shutting the door of our rented home. Silence. Then I hear a sound coming from her bedroom. She pops her head out, hair a mess.

"Hey," she smiles, trudging out and heading for the kitchen. "I need coffee something awful. What happened with that woman?"

Following her and gearing up for a battle, I say on a deep exhale, "Jason's taking her to a rehab now. It'll be her first one, I think."

"Oh good," Simone says without the slightest emotional investment as she reaches for the French press and opens a bag of ground coffee from Kroger.

"I told her about Nathan."

Simone smiles, but her mind is elsewhere. Is she already mad at me? There's a distance between us that's not normally there.

Maybe that's just me projecting because of what I have to share with her.

I am not looking forward to this.

Leaning against the counter I watch her fill a pot with water and turn one of the electric burners on. "Simone, I have to talk to you about something."

"Hey, Sarah," a deep voice greets me from behind. I quickly turn my head, my eyes widening at seeing Justin trudging out of her bedroom, shirtless in his suit-slacks, barefoot, his hair a mess, too. "Have a good time last night?" he asks me, crossing to Simone and pressing his body against her backside.

Meeting my eyes with the smile of a cat who ate twelve canaries she tilts her head back for a kiss that makes me want to throw up.

"What the fuck?" I mutter.

As Justin opens the fridge and pulls out bottled water, Simone shrugs and fake-whispers, "Ooopsie."

Now I'm worried. "What the hell is going on here?"

She holds up her hand, eyes sharpening. "Please, you don't get to judge me, boyfriend stealer."

My jaw drops and fear twists my heart. "What did you just call me?"

"I know you're in love with Jason. I have eyes. Remember? I told you I see a lot more than you think I see.

You've been lusting after him for months. Do you really believe I didn't know that's why he was able to get you so angry? Because you were interested in him the whole time!"

Feeling very trapped I blurt, "I didn't know it! I wasn't thinking of him that way until –"

" –It doesn't matter when! You were. And he was with me. And now he wants you, so that makes you a fucking backstabbing, boyfriend-stealing bitch!"

She may as well have just punched me with a hammer for how bad this hurts. "Simone."

Getting in my face with her index finger jabbing the air, she snarls, "Don't *Simone* me, Sarah."

All of those times I've kept my mouth shut when I didn't agree with what she was doing erupt in a volcano of unleashed resentment. Screaming, I tell her what I really feel. "You have no right to be mad at me! You told me – many times! – that Jason meant nothing to you! You have everything: talent, beauty, people supporting you, and you're so spoiled that when one person – one person! Out of how many fans do you have on social media? – decides he doesn't want to be treated like a temporary toy anymore you made it your goal to get him back, only with the intention of throwing him away again! Just to show him what he was missing??!!! Are you fucking kidding me right now? Who does that? How much adoration do you need, Simone? How big is your fucking ego? I mean, really?!!" Her jaw tightens and tears jump to her eyes, but I'm not done yet. "I haven't ever wanted anyone before. I've kept myself a fucking nun so I wouldn't get hurt again. I've only had sex with that one guy, and you know what he said to me after we were done? That he'd blown it because now *you* would never have sex with him!" Off her shock, I nod. "Yeah, he dated me to get to you. And fucked me because he was drunk. Do you know how that made me feel? I didn't tell you that because I didn't need you feeling sorry for me. But I am tired of standing back so you can have it all. If you wanted Jason – really wanted him in your heart – I wouldn't even have thought about him in that way. He would have been like an androgynous doll to me. Completely off limits. But you didn't want him! And you told me! And I saw it! And I saw him, and what a good guy he was, and yes, my feelings grew. But they *never* would have if you were in love with him. Which, from your sleeping with his fucking brother the first chance you get – just to prove you're wanted – just made really clear you don't care about Jason at all!"

Struggling for something to come back at me with Simone snaps, "Well, you slept with Jason last night so you obviously don't love me!"

Choked up and in so much pain for fighting with the woman who is in all forms but blood my sister, I step back and hold my head in my hands before I explode, "I didn't have sex with him! I wanted to! Boy, did I want to. But I had to talk to you, first. Because that's how much I care about you, even more than him or myself." Glancing to Justin, who's leaning against a wall and watching us from a quiet place, I shake my head. "No, that's not true. It's for myself that I didn't. Because I wouldn't have been able to look in a mirror had I not told you first how I felt about him."

Tears slide down Simone's cheek, the water pot boiling and forgotten behind her.

"Sarah…"

"I'm staying in Atlanta for a little while."

Shockwaves crash through her body and face. "He asked you to stay?"

Nodding, I whisper, because I still can't believe it, "Yes. He did." My eyes flit to Justin, but he betrays no emotion. He's going to make a great politician.

Simone looks over and turns the burner off, her fingers shaking. "I'm surprised."

"I bet," I bite back.

She frowns, her face still in profile.

Heading for my purse and the car keys beside it, I mutter, "I need some air."

32

JASON

The door to my loft opens. I call out from the bathroom, my mouth full of toothpaste, "In here!"

Justin appears behind me and leans on the doorframe, crossing his arms. "You haven't brushed your teeth yet today? Oh…coffee breath."

"Mmmhmm." I spit and run the faucet water over my toothbrush, sizing him up through the mirror. "Is that the same thing you wore last night?"

"I fucked Simone."

I freeze and blink at him, then flip off the tap and turn around. "What the fuck?"

His jaw moves around as he thinks a moment, bringing his eyes back to meet mine. "I wanted to help."

Narrowing a glare on him I toss the toothbrush onto the counter and cross my arms over my t-shirt, mirroring him.

"You're kidding me, Justin. I know you're a dick but wow."

His gaze drops to the floor as he says, "We've shared girls before."

Scoffing I snap, "Not to manipulate them!"

He nods and looks at me, parroting in a quieter tone, "No, not to manipulate them." Shoving his hands in his pockets he spreads his feet and exhales. "Look, I didn't like her. I wanted her gone. And I thought it was the way to do it. But Sarah handled it better than I did."

I know my brother's morals aren't always on the up and up. I said it before, he has a dark side. He's also a man who won't let anyone get in the way of what he wants. If what he wants has something to do with me, he'll do whatever it takes to make it happen, even if those actions are what I would deem wrong.

But now that he's mentioned Sarah with that look on his face, I'm dying of curiosity.

"How so?"

"She came clean. Told Simone off. It was harsh, but true. Needed to be said." His voice loses volume as he adds, "I should have done that instead."

On a laugh of pure disbelief, I mutter, "Well, it's too late for that now. How is Simone?"

"Smitten."

"Oh shit," I groan.

Justin moves over so I can get out of this bathroom. I need to pace. He leans against a wall and waits.

Finally, I grumble, "You deserve this. You deserve each other."

"I don't have feelings for the girl."

"I know! Jesus, you should have thought of that."

"How did I know she'd get all goo-goo eyed?!" he explodes.

Laughing harshly, I face him. "Because you're an asshole. Women like her love dark clouds! It's why she didn't like me. You're over there acting like you don't care, because you don't! And that is going to make her want you. God, you know this! It's science! It's how they work!"

"I know," he sighs loudly through his nose, looking very much like our father. "I'm going to…ah fuck. I don't know. What do you want me to do?"

I rub my forehead for solutions. "She lives in Detroit. Let it play out. Give it some time. Show her attention and don't hurt her. Let distance be the reason it ends." Off his look, I point at him. "I know what you're thinking. But she's not a bad person. She's just spoiled. She doesn't need you fucking with her heart right now when she's got this album coming out. It's more important than you. Hell, it's more important than her, too."

He makes a face like he doesn't understand.

But he wouldn't. Only an artist would. And the people who support them. Like me.

"Art isn't just for the person who made it. It's for the world."

Snorting, Justin mutters, "Write a Hallmark card."

Walking to my kitchen I almost don't spell it out for him, but this is something I'm passionate about, and I had to listen to his potholes speeches.

Over my shoulder while I pour orange juice for both of us, I tell him something that will probably never stick, but fuck it. I have to do this.

"The reason it's a tragedy when an artist dies at an early age, or why we all mourn David Bowie even when he lived a long life and leaves us, is because their art was sent to us, the people, to elevate our worlds. Make our days better. Life is shitty most of the time, and then there's that perfect song that moves your body and makes you forget your past, your future, everything." Justin has walked over and I hand him his juice as I finish, looking him right in his eyes, "Simone was given a gift. And her and those boys singing that song are going to lift people up when they hear it. And she's going to tour, and every city she goes to will be elevated by the people who bought those tickets. Because that's why art is so important. And you breaking her heart right now by telling her you don't care about her, isn't the right thing to do. You want to make this right? Treat her with respect. And let time take its course."

He's listened to every word, and he licks his lips against the ego-hit it is for him to take my advice. Justin was born two minutes before I was and believes in his heart that he's older than I am, and therefore should be leading the way. And he usually does. But sometimes, like today, I have to step into the older brother role.

He taps his juice glass to mine and nods once, muttering, "Okay."

"Good. Now go home and shower. I have to call Sarah."

As soon as the door clicks behind him I'm dialing the number I used to hate calling. She answers after three rings, right as I think I'm being sent to voicemail.

"Hello?"

"Hey," I smile. "Thought for a second you weren't going to answer."

I can hear the amusement in her reply. "I thought about it."

"You should've made me wait."

"I don't feel like playing games with you, Jason."

"Me neither." We're silent a moment and then I say, "What's on your schedule for today? I know how tight you keep that thing."

"I have to take Simone to the airport. Then I guess I'm coming back to the Airbnb."

"She's leaving?"

Lowering her voice, Sarah tells me, "Something happened I'm not sure it's my right to tell you."

"She slept with my brother."

"You know?"

Frowning I pick at a bubble of paint on my wall. "He just left. Yeah. He told me."

On a sigh, Sarah says, "Oh good. I didn't want that between us. How are you?"

"Fine."

"Really?"

"I don't have feelings like that for her, Sarah. Justin didn't hurt me with what he did."

Another exhale. "Oh good. Well, I know how he is, so I'm sure you won't mind my coming out and being honest. Simone's getting out of town so he doesn't get attached."

I almost snort, but instead mutter an incredulous, "Come again?"

"Yeah, he was really into her and she's just not feeling it. And after what I told her today when I was mad, she confessed she doesn't want to use men anymore. She'd rather just be alone for a little while."

"Ahh...well, I'm sure he'll be crushed, but he'll get over her in time."

Sarah's voice is weighted as she agrees, "I think the distance will help, don't you?"

I'm trying so hard not to laugh. "Yep. I hope you're right."

"Me too. She always leaves a string of broken hearts behind her and I don't want your brother hurting. Justin can be arrogant, but...you know."

"When can I see you?"

"Oh, uh," she laughs, nervous. "I can come by after the airport?"

"Come to the studio. I'll be working."

We get off the phone and I pull up my brother's number, thumb hovering. "Fuck it. I won't tell him. I'm gonna enjoy this too much. Maybe it'll teach him a lesson."

Laughing to myself, I dial Jake's number instead.

"Hey Jason, how was the party?"

"Weird. How's Drew?"

"Better. Fever broke. She's sleeping."

"Jake, Bernie showed up last night."

"Oh, fuck, you're kidding me? You toss her on her ass?"

Huffing through my nose as I head to pull the sheets off my bed for the laundry, I tell him, "No, that's why I'm calling. Tell Drew she finally agreed to rehab. I just got back from taking her there. Who knows if it'll stick, but it's the first time she agreed to go."

"Wow, okay, Drew'll want to know about this. She'll probably go visit."

"No visitors for awhile. It's going to be a rough start for her." I opt not to tell him about the heroine, and say instead, "But I have faith. When you and Drew go, I'll go with you guys, okay?"

"Sure. How'd you get her to say yes?"

Smiling as I tug the pillowcase off, I tell my brother with a big smile, "Sarah got her to go."

"Who's Sarah?"

"Someone you're about to meet. Very soon."

His voice lightens as he understands what I'm saying. "Holy shit, Jason! Are we talking BBQ time?"

"We most certainly are!"

33

JASON

No matter how many times I listen to their singing as I mix the tracks on *Just For Me*, it hasn't gotten old. I've got a half-eaten apple beside my soundboard, and an empty Styrofoam carton from take-out I picked up from Nuevo Laredo, the best Mexican restaurant in Atlanta. I had a craving for salmon tacos and they really rock them out there.

But even with my stomach satisfied, and the song moments away from being finished, I can't stop shifting in my chair looking at the clock, even though I never asked Sarah when she was coming, or when that flight took off.

When a light rapping comes from outside I mutter, "Finally," and spring up to let her in. Swinging the door open, sunlight hits me but it's far less powerful than the impact of seeing her for the first time since she left this morning. She looks tentative and soft. That crooked smile is killing me it's so cute. She's wearing flats so I bend down really low to make her laugh as I ask, "How's the weather down here."

"Ha! Shut up."

"Oh, cold I see. So much warmer up here. I'll just go back up."

She smacks my arm. "Jerk."

"Jerk?" I grab her and throw her over my shoulder. She yelps in surprise and starts hitting my ass with her fists as I kick the door shut. "This jerk is much stronger than you, little lady. Better be nice or I'll punish you." I give her ass a spank and make her yelp again.

"Jason, put me down!"

"Say please!"

"Put me down *now*!"

"Nah, how about I give you a little spin?" She starts yelling for me to stop as I whip us around in circles.

"I get carsick!"

Laughing I take her off my shoulder and slide her down my body, nice and slow. Fuck she feels good, but I love to mess with her so I say, "That's because you have control issues. No one ever gets carsick in the driver's seat."

"It's a chemical thing," she argues, eyes stubborn as she slips her arms around my waist and then surprises me by grabbing my ass and squeezing really hard. "Always wanted to do that," she grins.

My smile disappears as I lean down to kiss her. She pulls away before I can and whispers, "I'm having a really hard time with this."

"With what? Staying here with Simone gone?"

Her eyes are so vulnerable right now, the wall completely down. "Believing it's true."

I take her chin and press my lips to hers, holding there a moment before I say, "It's true."

She opens for me, her tongue lightly touching mine at first. Then she lets me lead the kiss into a hungrier one. My hands roam her body, but I can feel her resistance so I don't touch her breasts yet. Even though I'm dying to.

I keep kissing her until she starts moaning in my mouth and pressing her hips tighter against me like she wants more. I slip my hand under her t-shirt and her breath hitches in anticipation. Again I get the feeling she's inexperienced. Her eagerness has an innocence I haven't come across in a long time.

I run my finger under the wire of her bra as I lick her tongue, pressing my lips harder into hers as I reach all the way under and cup her breast, running my thumb over her nipple until it pebbles under my fingerprint. "Jason," she moans into my lips, sending shivers down my abs. My cock is so full it's painfully pushing at my jeans. They've shrunk. I'm straining to break free of them now.

"God, you taste so good," I groan as I work rougher kisses down her neck, caressing and pawing her other breast, both of my hands in heaven. "Let's take this off," I rasp. Her eyes go nervous as I pull her shirt over her head. "Haven't you done this before, Sarah?"

She licks her lips like she doesn't know if she should tell me.

I toss the fabric and free her breasts from her bra, tossing that, too. "Fuck, these are perfect." Leaning down I take one in my mouth. She arches her back and moans. Against her taut crest I murmur, "You can be honest. I can handle it."

On a whisper, she confesses to me, "Only once. And it was awful."

I look up from her nipple, lick it a few times while holding her eyes to smirk, "Well, then I'm about to blow your mind."

She bursts out laughing. "You're such a cocky fucker, Jason! I swear, can you have a little bit of modesty?!!"

My answer is rising up and devouring her. Lifting her while wrapping her legs around my hips. Grabbing her ass and grinding my erection onto her pussy, which I know is pulsing hard for my cock right now.

She moans into my mouth.

I growl back.

She bites my lip and I nearly go insane.

Pushing her against the wall I grind our bodies together and massage her naked breasts while lashing tongues with her until she's gasping for air and panting like she might cum just from this. With her legs locked around me I yank my shirt off and am about to kiss her, but the way she's looking at my chest stops me. I grin and she glances up to meet my eyes, hers full of shock laced with lust.

"What are you thinking right now?"

"I want to eat you alive," she whispers.

I lose the smile. "I know the feeling." Setting her down, I spin her around so fast that she slaps the wall to stabilize herself. I yank down her jeans over her ass, pulling the thong partially down with it. Hooking my finger under its lacey strap I slide it down her hips while chewing my way down her skin as each inch is revealed.

"What are you doing?" she moans.

Wrapping my arm around both her legs, I lift her off the ground and tear the pants and panties off, throwing them to the side. Then both her legs get spread and I arch her ass out and shove my face in it, reaching my tongue to her pussy to taste her for the first time. She makes the sexiest surprised sound, moaning as I work her. To add to her pleasure I stroke her folds with eager fingers, searching for and finding her sensitive and hard, tiny bean.

"You're so wet," I growl. She's panting now, and begging me to stop. "You really want me to?"

"Noooooo." She bends over more and gives me full access to her cunt from behind. "I'm just a little stunned. Keep going!"

I hold her thigh with one of my hands, rubbing it in rhythm to my licks, sliding the fingers of my other hand around her folds while I eat her out. I keep teasing her clit like I'm not coming back for it, then flicking it until she fucking starts screaming.

"Oh my God! Oh Jesus!"

Her pussy begins contracting around my tongue and she's so wet and ready for more that I just might blow right now I'm so turned on. I cup her and tongue her while she cums, stretching out her screams until she goes boneless with me having to catch her.

"Your mouth is all shiny," she smiles up at me as I carry her to my couch.

"Yeah, well, someone got excited," I growl, eager to fuck her. I wish I was the first, but I'm glad I'm the second and that he sucked. I want to be the only one who made her scream like that. And I plan on doing it again right now.

Setting her down gently I straighten up I gaze at her naked body, her eyes hooded, lips curved in a happy smile.

Feeling an ache in my chest at how much I care for

her, I rasp, "You're beautiful."

Her face twists up and she covers it with her small hands. "Don't lie to me."

I bend to pull her hands off. "Hey, I wouldn't lie about that. You're beautiful. You are."

"No, Simone's beautiful," she moans, turning her face so I can't see her.

Fuck. That. Shit.

I climb on top of Sarah, straddling her, my jeans and sneakers still on. Gently turning her face to make her look into my eyes I tell her, "Sarah, I don't want Simone. I want you. I'm falling in love with you."

Tears spring to her eyes and she blinks at me. "Don't say that if you don't mean it, Jason."

"You're going to find how much I mean it," I whisper, bending to kiss her. She ropes her arms around my neck and rises up, returning my kisses while tears fall down her cheeks. I can feel them and they're killing me.

If I could go back in time I would have picked her. And I'm going to do everything in my power from this day forward to make that right.

She reaches for my zipper and I start laughing. "Well now, who's eager?"

Grinning she says, "I want to see the reason you're so full of yourself."

"Oh yeah? You think you're ready for this?"

"Totally," she shoots back. "Can't wait."

Jumping off the couch and hard as ever, I kick off my sneakers and yank my socks off.

"Jeez," she says with a roll of her eyes. "Why is this taking so fucking long? Stalling?"

Forcing myself to stop laughing, I cock an eyebrow. "My socks aren't sexy. I want you to have the full impact when you see me naked for the first time. I want it to really hit you like you're seeing the Grand Canyon or Stonehenge."

"Oh my God," she groans. "You're too much. I mean, really. This has been fun but I think I've changed my mind."

I unzip my pants, push them down and step out of them. I was going commando. So I'm completely on display for her now.

Her mouth drops open and her eyes go wide. "Holy shit," she whispers.

"Watch this," I grin, laying my hand near my naked cock and using the thick muscle to bounce it onto my palm. "It does tricks."

She covers her mouth and rises on her knees. Through her fingers she shouts, "What the hell am I going to do with that thing?! You're fucking enormous!!"

I start walking to her, offering my throbbing erection in my hand.

"Well, if you want to leave now, I'm not stopping you."

Sarah surprises the hell out of me by sliding off the couch and kneeling in front of my body, reaching for my dick with open lips. "You don't have to do that…" I begin but my words choke off as she takes me into her mouth, grabbing the base since she couldn't possibly take it all in on the first try.

I groan and sway as she licks and sucks me.

My veins start pulsing and goosebumps shoot down my abs as she reaches for my balls and lightly cups them.

"Holy shit," I moan.

She keeps going and she's pretty fucking good.

"How do you know how to do that?"

She shuts me right up by moaning on my cock and touching her index finger to the skin just behind my sack. I groan and feel the surge begin, the heat that sets me throbbing like I'm going to shoot everything into her mouth before I'm ready to.

"Stop! Stop. God."

But she just moves faster.

I have to pull away from her panting lips. "That's it. I have to fuck you."

Almond colored eyes gaze at me with shameless lust and I swear I've never seen anything sexier. I grab her, toss her on the couch and fight the urge to fuck her doggy style. It's our first time. She's barely had sex in her life. I'm going to do this face-to-face so no hidden insecurities come out and fuck this up for us. Hovering over her I look into her eyes and say, "Hey."

She smiles and touches my face. "Hi Jason."

Sliding my hand between her legs I groan as she spreads them for me, giving me access. "I want you so badly, Sarah."

"Then take me."

Growling, I kneel between her thighs and stroke her slippery cunt a few times, really slow with my thumb as I kiss her. Our tongues dance as I push my hips in, touching the blunt tip of my cock to her opening. Rising up to watch her face, I begin to penetrate her, slowly thrusting in and hissing through gritted teeth. "You're so tight," I moan, trying not to move too quickly yet.

She's grimacing slightly as her walls expand to allow me entry. Licking her lips she searches my face, her breasts rising in halting breaths.

"Relax, Sarah. I'm here with you."

She nods and a tear slips down her cheek. "I don't cry!"

"I don't see any tears," I murmur.

She grins briefly because she knows I saw it and lied,

then her frown comes back as I go deeper in.

"You're so big!"

"You want me to go slower?"

"I want you to go faster!"

Chuckling, I rasp, "Then here we go." I start to move the way I want to, plunging in a little deeper every time. I can feel her body start to relax more and open with the pleasure, and her back arches on a sexy moan.

"Oh my God! Jason!" she cries out, clawing my back as I finally dive in all the way to the hilt, pushing her leg open more with one of my knees. I grab her breast and flick the crest with my thumb while groaning and closing my eyes as I ram her without forgiveness.

As she cums on my cock she starts screaming, the sound so sexy my eyes roll back in my head. The pulsing of her orgasm is so good that all I can see is white-hot heat again. My thighs start throbbing and my cock starts to burn with its release. She claws her way up and grabs my head, kissing me as I cum, body jerking with hers.

"Fuck!" I groan into her lips. "You're so fucking tight, Sarah, Jesus, I can't stop cumming." She grinds her pussy and hips into me and I shout, "Holy shit!" and collapse on her as she rains kisses all over my jaw.

Our chests are rising in harmony as we catch our breath, panting and gasping for air. "I'm sorry," I whisper.

"For what?"

Burrowing into her soft, curly red hair I murmur, "For not seeing you earlier. I'm sorry." She strokes my head with her nails and doesn't say anything. She doesn't need to. She just needed to listen. Nothing she could say right now would make this moment any more perfect.

34

SARAH

Rolling over in Jason's bed I stretch my arm to search for him before opening my eyes. When I feel his side empty, I crack a groggy glance around and see I'm alone. Stretching my body like a cat feels so good after the workout that man's been giving me. I keep waiting for him to get tired, but it's been three days and we've only gotten out of bed to eat and shower.

Sounds from the kitchen travel over the divider wall and I smile, listening to him humming as he cooks breakfast. "What's better than waking up to the smell of bacon?" I call out.

With mock-seriousness he calls back, "Waking up to the smell of my cock!"

Laughing I throw the cover off and walk out, buck naked. He's naked, too, and looking gorgeous as ever. "I knew you were going to say that, Jason."

"You set 'em up, I'll knock 'em down," he smirks, using a fork to turn strips over in order to brown them to a nice crisp. His eyes rest several hot moments on my bouncing breasts and he breathes in through his teeth a sexy hiss.

I might have made this walk a little bouncier than normal.

It's been heaven to feel his hungry looks lighting me up. They've freed me to walk around like this without insecurity. I'm average looking. Cute, maybe. But Jason makes me feel beautiful just as I am. Not just with his saying it, which he's done several times at the most unexpected moments, but by how he looks at me.

No one has ever looked at me the way he does.

"Still sore, babe?"

Nodding, I murmur, "Mmhmm. But I don't mind."

"Come over here," he growls.

I hurry over to his side and he slides his free hand between my legs. My tummy clenches with desire immediately. He's conditioned this response. Dampness is just my way of life now. I'm going to have to buy extra panties.

As he teases my pussy I moan at his skill. Can't be jealous of any of the girls from his past because they've made him the talent he is today.

He fingers my clit, sliding the pad of his middle finger

slowly over it, then picking up speed on the side he's discovered is my most sensitive.

I grab onto the counter and bend forward over the bread he's laid out for toasting. He moves his hand around the back and reaches under my ass, slipping two digits inside my pussy. I arch and moan, closing my eyes in ecstasy.

"Faster, Jason."

"Dirty tiny bitch, that's what you are."

I moan, "Fucking damn right," craning my ass up higher by rising on my tiptoes.

Jason groans, but keeps poking the bacon with a fork as he fucks me with three fingers now. "Shit, Sarah, you're making the bacon look boring."

Panting I shake my head, "Bacon's never boring."

He chuckles and pushes his fingers really deep, touching my g-spot. I cry out and rub against his palm. "Cum for me, Sarah. That's right, you greedy little nemesis."

Laughing I wiggle against his fingers until a high-pitched moan escapes my core. I slap my palms on the counters as he pushes my orgasm over the edge with the hottest, rough thrusts of his digits. The sounds he's making, his breath hitching, the masculine groans as he watches me break wide open for him are so fucking hot I want more.

"Fuck me," I growl.

He chuckles, "I'm cooking."

"Fuck me right now or you'll never see me again."

"Well, since you put it that way." He tosses the fork in the sink, tearing his sweats down his thighs, coming behind me and ramming into me so hard and fast I cry out from the ache. I'm so sore from the fuck-fest we've been having but it's a delicious feeling to be filled by him when my pussy is still trembling with aftershocks. I'm loving every single fucking second of this.

He snarls through gritted teeth, "Happy now?" as he grips my ass and fucks me from behind.

"No! Harder!"

"Jesus, you're so fucking hot," he groans. "And you're going to get what you asked for you."

"Call me a bitch again."

He grabs my hair and pulls my head back to growl in my ear, "How about I call you a cunt?" slamming his whole glorious length into me, balls deep.

"Say *cunt* again, Jason, you fucking cocky bastard."

He groans in my ear and I feel his girth thicken inside me. "Sopping wet tight little…cunnnnntttt. Eating me whole. Begging for more."

"Yes," I moan. "Keep going."

"Sarah, I should have known you liked it rough."

"Harder!"

He chuckles in my ear, grabs my thighs and lifts me off

the ground. I'm holding onto the counter like I'm Superman spread eagle flying through the air.

"This is crazy!" I start laughing.

He starts cracking up, too, then moves a little slower. The sensation of his full shaft penetrating me when I'm this slippery and excited is so amazing I start to moan. He lets out a primal sound and growls, "I'm cumming in like two seconds."

"Me too." The burning tingles begin to spread and travel all the way down my legs and up my chest as the orgasm approaches. He keeps moving nice and slow, dragging out the agony of nearing ecstasy. I start moaning, sucking in my breath and quivering all over. Jason gets harder right before he cums and that sends me right over the edge.

He roars and starts panting, "I can feel you cumming, baby! Yes! Holy fuck! Yes!"

"Ooooohhhh," I whimper, knuckles white, everything tense as he pours all of his semen into me until it spills over.

When he lowers my legs I can't even stand up. I start to collapse but he catches me in time, pulling me against his hard body.

He grunts, "Let's go out for breakfast."

I glance over and see the bacon is charred to black. "Mmhmm."

He chuckles and kisses the top of my hair.

"Finally got you to shut up."

"I hate you."

"I hate you, too."

35

SARAH

"What are you doing here?" Simone says as I walk into our apartment.

Gripping the key in my hand I shut the door with finality. "Well, I called you every day for a whole two weeks and you never picked up or called me back. So, here I am."

"Maybe I don't want to talk to you!" she snaps with an eye roll from the couch. She's balled up with her knees close to her chest, HBO's *Girls* playing on the T.V. with the sound cranked up.

I lay my purse down, walk over and watch for a moment. "You're re-watching season two?"

With her tone dead she mutters, "Yes."

Plopping onto our couch beside her, I let time pass without either of us talking. We've seen all these episodes together. This is a sign that she misses me. Also, she's not told me to get the fuck out yet.

When the end credits play, I whisper, "I'm sorry."

She sucks on her lips and mutters, "Me too."

We reach for each other's hands at the same time and clasp them, holding for a moment before letting go. "How're things with Justin?"

"I finally had to tell him I'm not interested last night. He called me every day. It was really annoying. Between the two of you my phone wouldn't stop ringing."

On a smile, I knock her shoulder with mine. "Must be tough being loved."

All the air leaves her lungs and she squeezes her knees in closer, laying the side of her cheek on them to look at me. "I've been lost, Sarah. I didn't realize how much you did everything for me until you were gone."

Pain twists my heart up. "Yeah."

"You've done a lot!"

"Yep. But in all fairness, you paid me."

"Not as much as I should have."

Smiling ruefully, I remind her, "I do your books — you paid what you could. We just always knew I'd make an actual living when you hit it big."

"I know," she murmurs, holding my eyes. "And that's going to happen now. How're things with you and Jason?"

"Good. It feels weird you asking me that question."

She shrugs. "Yeah, but oh well. How's it going?"

"Good. He told me he sent you the finished album."

"He did. Did you hear it?"

Shaking my head I confess, quietly, "I thought you should hear it first. Didn't feel right. I'm normally with you, and it's your music, so…no."

"Want to hear it now?"

Smiling with relief and love in my heart, I nod as tears threaten. "Yeah. I'd like that."

She leans in with a funny look like she can't believe her eyes. "Are you going to cry? You never cry!"

"I cried when I heard the choir. Kind of."

And with Jason, several times. And several others on my own when I was overwhelmed with how lucky I feel now that he's with me. But I'm keeping that to myself.

She smiles, not willing to drop it. "Ahhh! You got all gooshy since you left. Look at Sarah the badass, all soft and smooshy!"

"Shut up!" I laugh.

She reaches over and tickles me. "Sarah's in loooooove!"

"I am not," I cry out, jumping off the couch. "And I hate being tickled."

"I know," she grins. Then her smile fades and her eyes become serious. "I'm happy for you."

With parted lips I try to say something, but I can only

give this awkward little nod.

She gets off the couch and strolls in her pajama shorts and t-shirt to her laptop, powering it on and leaning an elbow on the counter, her long blonde hair draped over the keys. "I haven't listened to it yet, either." Glancing to me, she shrugs one shoulder. "I've been kind of depressed since our fight."

"Why didn't you call me back so we could make up?"

"I needed some time. You said some things about me —"

"—I know. I was mean."

"You were right." She holds my look. "I've been doing some soul-searching. I don't want to be selfish like that anymore." The screen lights up her face and she straightens up to hit play. Hovering an index finger over the Return key, she shows me all her teeth in a nervous grimace. "Eek. Oh God. Ready?"

"Ready!" I run over.

We listen to the whole album, all ten songs, and by song number two we're dancing around our living room singing along with it, sometimes really loudly, sometimes whispers with our hands up like we're squirrels.

When *Just For Me* begins we both scream and run to the computer, even though there's nothing on the screen but the title and album cover.

We go silent as her voice comes out of the speakers.

And when the boys join her, I grab her arm and she grabs mine.

Tears are in our eyes. We know we're witnessing something people are going to love so much!

Jason did an amazing job layering the harmonies. A portion of the tracks she completed before the choir recording drift over the middle of the boy's chorus and neither she nor I knew he was going to do that.

"Oh my God," she breathes, meeting my eyes.

I nod that I love it, too, and we stay like this until the song ends.

"You're going to be a superstar," I whisper, with tears in my eyes.

Her blue eyes are liquid, too. Her face squishes with emotion and she croaks, "If I don't have you in my life I don't care about any of it. You're my family, Sarah."

That's it. Complete waterworks. The floodgates break and I can't even see her anymore. "You're mine, too!"

We hug and I pull away, wiping my tears with my hand as she sniffles.

"Simone, I…"

"You're moving to Atlanta, aren't you?"

Nodding through tears, I gasp for air and squeak, "Yes."

"But you can come to my shows. And we have

Facetime. And I can visit you guys."

"Would you? I'd love to come to your shows!"

She hugs me again, this time harder, whispering in my ear. "Oh thank God. Because you've been at every one I've ever had! If you weren't there…I don't know how I'd go on without you gripping some stupid curtain in suspense!"

I start laughing and pull away from the hug. "Okay, no more hugs. I can't take all this girliness."

Simone laughs, her cheeks all wet. "Good to see he hasn't completely changed you."

Snorting I wave her off. "Pffth. He hasn't changed me at all."

Wiping both sides of her face with flattened fingers she cocks her head and says, "Really? Because you're about five pounds skinnier than when I saw you last."

Blushing I glance down to my body. It's true that my jeans are bordering on baggy. I had to wear a belt for the first time with these.

"I'm the same!" I lie.

"Uh-huh," she rolls her eyes. "It's okay. It's too weird to talk about."

"It is."

36

JASON

"What the fuck, Sarah?"

"What?" she asks, eyeballing me from her profile.

"Don't you own anything?" I'm staring at the boxes that were shipped to my loft. There are only three.

Throwing her fists on her hips she faces me with a challenge. "I'm low maintenance. Would you prefer I have a shit-ton of shoes? Would that make you happy so you could categorize me in some box you have assigned for the human female?"

Laughing under my breath, I throw my arms up. "Alright! Fine. You travel light. I get it." Lifting the largest one from where the U.P.S. guy left it, I groan under the weight. "Jesus, what's in here?"

"Books."

"Just books?"

"And three photo albums. Heave ho, buddy. Those

muscles ought to be good for something."

I chuckle, "Don't make me laugh while I'm carrying the entire Detroit library here."

She grabs hold of the medium sized box and drags it further into my loft, announcing as if she's lived here forever, "We need shelves."

Fuck, I am so crazy about her. The two weeks she was gone was fucking torture for me. We talked on the phone daily but as I told her multiple times, not being able to kiss her was a living hell. I'd just figured out how important she was to my happiness, and then she had to go and leave.

Because fighting with her is most of the fun, I groan, "Shelves? Why? They're stupid."

"Because, jerk face, my books need a home and...oh my God!"

I grin, lowering the box in front of a mounted bookcase I got for her. It was delivered today from Amazon while she was out buying two planters for the succulents she forced me to buy from Trader Joes on Monroe in Midtown. The girl went crazy for their flowers, but then decided to get something that would last longer. I told her there weren't enough windows in the loft for the things. She insisted if they lived outside they'd survive. And then she borrowed my Escalade — alright, she stole it while I was napping — to get larger pots for the damn plants. And a good thing, too, because that's when I got the knock on the door. It gave me enough time to put this shelf together.

Sometimes things just work out.

"Jason!"

"You like it?"

Her mouth is wide open and she's shaking her head in disbelief. "I love it! This is probably the nicest thing anyone has ever done for me! Holy crap!" She runs over and hugs me as hard as she can, which isn't very. Then she jumps back and admires the shelves with a huge grin. "Open the box so we can put the books on it right now! Oh my God, they're going to be so happy with their new home!"

I'm laughing at her freak-out, and secretly very pleased with myself for coming up with the idea. During one of our phone conversations she'd told me how much she likes to read, and that the main thing to ship were her books. I logged on the 'zon that evening.

Since I'm not making a move to unpack now, she rips the tape of the box to get started without me. I rush over, pick her up and spin her upside down like I'm going to shake her pockets for loose change. "Oh no, you don't, Sarah. No books now. You're not getting out of the family BBQ."

"Put me down! I'm serious about the car sickness. I'll throw up on you!"

Flipping her over and setting her down I hold her chin,

smiling at her flushed cheeks. "Go get ready."

"What should I wear?"

"They'll have heat lamps, but you get cold easily, so how about those grey jeans and a sweater. Do you have one?"

Rolling her eyes she tells me, "Of course I have a sweater. I'm from Detroit. Your winters are summers compared to our hell. Why do you think we're so tough?" Groaning and nervous, she goes back for the smallest box but I beat her there and open it with a couple strong rips. Digging in, she produces a brick red sweater that will look fucking awesome with her auburn hair. "This okay, Jason?"

"Hell yeah."

Wrapping her in my arms I lift her off her feet for a long kiss. She responds with as much passion, slipping her arms around my neck.

"I can't wait for you to meet my family, Sarah."

"I'm nervous," she whispers against my lips.

"You should be. They're very judgmental." Off her wide-eyed look, I laugh, "I'm fucking with you."

Her little nose squishes up. "You're not nice, Jason Cocker."

"And you are?"

37

SARAH

Truth? I have no idea what to expect. Jason has told me about his family. And of course I've met Justin, but that's all. Since I was enmeshed in Jason's professional life while working with Simone, I have little to go on.

I've never met this Jake he keeps talking about, or his new wife, Drew. I don't know Jaxson or the woman he proposed to a couple months ago. Jason talks about Jett like he's a superhero and has already warned me he'll be absent, traveling the states with his motorcycle club, The Ciphers. And Jeremy, well, Jeremy's in the Marines and everyone wishes the youngest of the Cocker Brothers was home safe — that's all I know. And that he looks like Jake, apparently. But to me, that means nothing since I have no reference point.

After Simone went back to Detroit, Jason and I stayed in his place for two weeks having sex and talking and keeping to ourselves while we got to know each other in this new way. The eight-hour days for four months while she was working on the album of course didn't seem to count. We needed time to just be us, and have fun together. And fuck like animals all over the damn loft and in his Escalade. I loved it. But the bubble had to burst sometime.

So I went home and healed my painful rift with Simone, and then took care of all that was needed for me to move.

I've been moved in with Jason for the past four days now, waiting for my shipment and handling Simone's career remotely with all the wonders modern technology has provided. Why offices still exist, I'll never know.

Then Jason planned this BBQ for tonight — a Saturday in November — and I am so anxious I want to call it off.

But of course I'm not a wimp and would never dare do that. BUT I WANT TO!!

"Ready?" Jason asks, coming out of his bathroom. Upon seeing him, my breath hitches because he's so handsome I can't believe he's my boyfriend. His hair is more styled than I've ever seen it, and his outfit is far less casual than normal. He's wearing black jeans and a pale-blue button-up underneath a soft grey sweater.

"Did you wear that grey sweater to match my jeans?"

He shrugs with a guilty smirk, "No, that'd be lame."

"You're very sweet," I murmur, walking over and rising on my toes to kiss him. "I'll go put heels on so I'm not so short."

"No."

Cocking my head I ask, "Why not?"

"Because I like you the way you are."

My heart melts and my face follows. "Awww!"

His eyes sparkle with amusement as he adds, "And the BBQ is on a lawn, so they'll sink in. Flats only."

Smacking his arm, I cry out, "Jerk. I thought you were being sweet for once."

"Nope," he chuckles, heading to grab a bottle of wine.

In the medium-sized box are my toiletries, extra hard drives, framed photos of me and Simone, and my five pairs of shoes. I grab my charcoal grey ballet flats and slip them on before joining him in the kitchen.

Holding up the bottle of chardonnay he explains, "Jaxson always brings red wine, so…"

"Gotcha." I blink as he stares at me in a weird way. "What?"

"Did you curl your hair?"

"My hair is naturally curly," I mutter.

"It looks different."

Sighing, I admit, "I got it styled today. Softer curls."

He grins, "That's why you took so long to get those fucking planters."

"I wanted to look nice!" I exclaim, throwing my hands up and walking away. "Sue me!"

Chuckling under his breath he follows me to the door. "I like it. You look adorable, baby."

Throwing him a glance over my shoulder, I mutter, "Meh."

"Try and be nice to them."

"You only wish."

38

SARAH

In Buckhead, which Jason tells me is the Beverly Hills of Atlanta, he parks his Escalade in front of a gorgeous home set deep inside a perfectly landscaped lawn that could fit two of the homes I grew up in.

I swallow hard.

"Wait there," he orders me.

I open the door, ignoring him. He arrives just in time to catch me jumping out.

"Sarah! I keep telling you. I'm going to open the door for you."

"That's stupid," I mutter, my eyes on the house. "I'm not an invalid."

"It's a sign of respect," he chuckles, closing my door and hitting the key fob to lock the vehicle as we walk toward the home he grew up in.

Inside there's a distant sound of conversations and he whispers to me, "They're in the backyard."

"Okay."

"Be very nervous."

"You're not helping."

He takes my hand and I glance to him as he gives my fingers a squeeze.

After the foyer we pass a living room that looks comfortable, not too perfect or museum-like. I begin to relax. There's a staircase on the left that has family photos on the wall of the boys when they were children and teenagers. "Ooooh, I want to look at those!"

Jason steers me over. "Okay, but just for a second. Everyone's waiting."

The frames begin at ground level then continue up the stairs' incline. First is a picture of the six boys together in front of a swimming pool, all with their shirts off and chests scrawny. "This is when we were six." He points to him and Justin, standing next to each other.

"You guys are so cute!" I whisper. "I love your red sneakers. And look at your little face! Awww."

"Can you tell which is me?"

Knocking my shoulder into his arm I scoff, "Of course. You're smiling and he looks like an asshole."

Jason cracks up. "He does. But that's only because he hated having his picture taken. And he wasn't shy about letting them know how he felt at all times." Pointing to the handsome boy furthest right, Jason says, "That's my oldest brother Jaxson, he'd be nine I think. His hair is a little darker now, but look at his eyes. Looks like an old man even then. You're about to meet Rachel, too, they were friends when this photo was taken. Before she moved away. But I told you their story." Jason smiles at me and points to the boy next to Jaxson, who's the same height but has a buzz cut and blonder hair. "That's Jett. A year younger than Jax and almost two years older than us."

"Your mom was busy."

Jason chuckles, "Yeah, she was."

"It's weird seeing you as a boy, Jason. And no tattoos. Which reminds me, what is the spiky one with the 'C' on your chest mean? Does it stand for Cocky?"

He smirks. "Nice one, babe. It stands for Cocker. All us brothers got that same tat as soon as we each turned eighteen." Smiling at the memory, he points to the two youngest boys. "That's Jake and that's Jeremy — see how they have darker hair and eyes than us. That's from my mom's side. The only ones with brown eyes like hers. Jeremy's grinning like a nut here, still wearing diapers under his swim trunks. Hahah! But he got real somber as he grew up."

"Why?"

Jason thinks about it, staring at the photo. "I dunno. Maybe because he's the youngest? Felt he had something to prove? The Marines sure did that. We've seen him on leave only once since he was shipped overseas. He's a fucking badass." Glancing to me, his eyes are wistful. "I can't wait for you to meet him."

"Me too."

"Oh yeah? Good, then let's do this!"

"More photos!"

"Quit stalling!"

He maneuvers me away from the stairs and I take a deep breath of resignation.

I feel like I'm in over my head today. My family isn't close like Jason's is. My dad left when I was five. My grandparents on his side didn't keep in touch with me or Nathan, which now that I'm older seems very cruel and the opposite of how grandparents are supposed to be. They must have been selfish people.

I'll never seek them out to find out why they abandoned us when he did. I'm too angry with them, because I secretly believe that's why my brother went down the wrong path so easily.

My mother and I aren't close. She was always very flighty. Found her worth in her men and had a string of boyfriends. She's happily married now, but it took six tries down the aisle. I just don't relate to her. It's why Simone became so important to me. And her family is similar to mine, so we clicked in a way we both needed.

The Cocker Family kitchen is gorgeous. It's bright, large and really tidy considering there's a party going on. The warm lighting looks brighter than normal against the waning evening light seen through the windows.

Through the glass door there's a backyard that is the largest I've ever seen, framed with oak trees along the sides and back instead of a fence.

Close to the back porch, on the flattest part of the grass, are twinkle lights set up with four poles as their base, four space heaters to match, all aglow and shining on the faces of a family deep in various conversations. To the left is a long cloth-draped table where food platters wait, as yet untouched. They're covered with netted gauze tents to keep bugs at bay.

Jason tightens his grip on my hand and opens the glass door with his elbow, since the white wine is in the way. People stop talking in a domino effect. Heads turn and my heart starts pounding.

Justin spotted us first. He rises up and announces like he has a megaphone, "Ladies and gentlemen, Jason is in love!"

"You suck," Jason calls out to his twin. "I haven't told her that yet! You're ruining the surprise!"

My face goes bright red, and everything tingles. He loves me?

Justin shouts through cupped hands, "As if they can't see it on your face."

With a lot of laughter people rise up to meet me. As Michael Cocker, the family patriarch, approaches, I want to run and hide. He's the epitome of dignity. And Jason's mom, Nancy, is clearly high-society. If they knew some of the things I'd witnessed chasing down my brother, or the smarmy boyfriends my mother brought home, they would not be impressed.

But as they shake my hand and smile, I feel no judgment from them, only friendliness and acceptance in their welcoming smiles. I relax immediately, smiling back as Jason beams.

"So nice to meet you, Sarah," Nancy Cocker says with genuine enthusiasm. "I wish I had your hair color!"

"I hated it, growing up," I confess.

She makes a face. "I hated mine, too. I had a friend named Gretchen who was strawberry blonde. Gorgeous. God I was so in love with her hair."

Grinning, I nod. "I know that feeling."

A very handsome, very well-built man in his mid-to-late twenties with brown eyes and dark hair steps forward with his hand out. "I'm Jake. I've heard a lot about you."

"I've heard a lot about you, too. And I just saw your photo inside."

"Not me on the pony," he groans, looking at Jason.

"No, I only showed her the first one, of us all together when we were little kids."

"Thank God," Jake smirks. "I hate that pony photo. This is Drew. My wife." He presents a pretty, dark-haired, blue-eyed woman with a sweet, Southern drawl.

"I heard about what you did for Bernie. So nice to meet you."

My eyes light up. "I'm so happy to meet you, too. Is she doing well?"

"She passed the twenty-eight day mark and she's still there so I'm hopeful this is it. Thank you."

"It wasn't my doing," I say, but Drew's face says she thinks I'm being modest.

A rugged man with suntanned skin and emerald eyes steps forward, his deep voice and calm demeanor cluing me in to who he must be before he even says, "I'm Jaxson." He shakes my hand so firmly my whole body feels it. "And this is my fiancé, Rachel."

A clear-eyed, pretty woman with sandy-brown hair, extends her hand. I'm starting to feel too professional with all the handshakes, so I just go for it and open my arms. She grins and hugs me. "Nice to meet you, Sarah."

"You too! Jason told me about what he did for you guys. So romantic."

"Oh, at the last BBQ?" she grins, taking Jaxson's hand. He leans down and gives her a soft kiss.

Jason's grandma shouts, "What about me?" with a twinkle in her eyes, waving me over from a chair with two cushions while the others have one.

Thankfully the party is small, so she's the last person I have to meet. Jett and Jeremy I knew wouldn't be here, and also Jason's cousins couldn't make it because of the impending hurricane — they were afraid of being stuck for several days, unable to return to Savannah in time for work.

Jason rests his hand on my lower back and guides me over to meet his grandmother as the family takes their seats. He says loudly enough for everyone to hear, "Be careful, Sarah. This is the final test. Grams is a hard ass."

Everyone yells at the same time, "Language!"

Grams said it, too, and she throws them all a dirty look. "That's my line!"

There's a lot of laughing, and then May Cocker gives me a scrutinizing gaze. "Well, you're a sight for old eyes."

"Hi Mrs. Cocker. I'm Sarah Daly."

She nods, humming, "Mmhm Mmhm," looking me up and down. "You're cute as a button!"

Blushing I glance to Jason. "You hear that? She thinks I'm cute."

"She doesn't know you," he winks to me, and to his

grandmother he fake-whispers, "Grams, she's making my life miserable."

Her smile grows and she nods with approval. "Good. My Jerald did the same to me, bless his soul. You'll never be bored."

Justin runs up, grabs and flips me over so that I have to hold my sweater in place to stay modest. "What? I don't get a hello? Am I invisible or something?"

"Oh my God! I hate twins!" I groan. "You're way too alike. Put me down!"

Justin goes and hands me off to Jason like I weigh less than a glass of water or something. "I believe this is yours."

"Why thank you. I'll take that." Jason sets me down and gives me a quick, happy kiss before we join the table.

I steal a lot of glances around as they all talk easily. Jason keeps his hand on my leg the whole time, laughing often as the brothers throw tons of verbal jabs at each other.

There's a warmth growing in my chest as the evening goes on. I'm beginning to feel like I could belong here.

We serve ourselves, buffet-style. When I taste Nancy's chili I close my eyes in heaven. "Mrs. Cocker, this is the best chili I've ever had in my life."

Nancy smiles with pride. To Jason she winks, "She really means that."

"You'll never catch Sarah lying, Mom."

"Well, then she can stay."

I'm grinning, but then Jason's face falls. "Whoa! Wait a minute! Stop everything!"

Everyone goes silent and looks over.

"Where's the ginger ale?" he demands.

With her fork full of chili, Grams informs him, "There isn't any this time."

"None of Mom's fresh ginger ale!?!" Jason cries out. "That's the first BBQ we've ever had where you didn't make any, mom!"

"Sorry, Jason. I wasn't in the mood," Nancy explains with a bored look.

His jaw drops. "You weren't…in the mood? What?" Looking around the table, he asks, "How are you all okay with this?"

Everybody shrugs.

Jake reaches under the table and produces a hidden pitcher. "Gotcha."

Loud laughter ripples through the party, but Jason looks like he might explode. "Fuck you, Jake."

"Language!" Grams yells, before she mutters, "Ha ha, beat you to it," with self-satisfaction glinting in her eyes.

When we all settle down and people go back to their conversations, Jason pours his cherished ginger-ale into my empty water glass. "You should feel honored I'm sharing this with you. I've been known to hoard it and drink it all."

I can't even talk, I'm so happy as I gaze at him.

He glances over and says in a quiet volume just for me, "What are you smiling at, shrimp cake?"

"I love you."

He freezes and puts the pitcher down to cup my chin and look into my eyes, his voice deep. "I love you, too, Sarah."

39

SARAH

Just over a year later.

"I don't care if you think it should be orange! Simone hates orange lights on her! They wash her out. Now change it to hot pink, with red and yellow accents, for variety."

The lighting engineer mutters, "Sorry, Sarah," running back to his station while I take quick strides backstage in the other direction.

We're at the Staples Center's concert hall in Los Angeles, and when I drove up in the Porsche Simone rented for me, fans were lined around the block.

Flying into her dressing room I discover her cross-legged on the floor in meditation. She opens one eye. "Calm down, Sarah. You look very stressed out."

"Calm down!? Over thirty-thousand people are here, most of them wearing a t-shirt with your face on it!"

"So?"

I start laughing like an insane person. "And the fucking engineer wanted to project orange lights through the gobos!"

With a voice of pure serenity she offers, "And you stopped him, because that's what you do."

I stare at her, face going blank. "I liked you better before you went all Zen."

She cocks an eyebrow and closes her eyes, facing front and holding her gorgeous neck long and centered. "Well I didn't. Now let me get back to meditating. I have twelve minutes."

On a half-laugh, I mutter, "Okay, do your thing," and head outside, closing the door a little too loudly. "Sorry!" I call through it and head off, checking my phone for how long it is before she goes on.

She was right, it was twelve minutes. And now it's eleven. But how she knew that is beyond me because she removed the clock from her dressing room saying it made her focus on the wrong things in life.

Because I'm not looking where I'm going I run right into Jason. "Hi!"

My head flies up and my jaw drops. "What are you doing here?"

He smirks, "Surprise!"

I jump into his arms and he swings me around, kissing me like crazy as he slides me down his body. "Oh Jason, I'm so glad you came!"

"Usher wanted to see the show so we paused working on his album and flew over…wait for it…in his private jet."

"Oh my God, you lucky bastard!"

"Plus he wanted to see his dancers do their thing."

"It was very nice of him to refer them to us since he's not touring." Just as I say that, Rue and Jenna come running over in the cutest red-leather pants and grey halters, plus Converse sneakers made with special grips for sliding on the stage.

"Sarah! Thomas is puking," Rue blurts out, then, "Hi Jason."

Jenna explains, "He got drunk before the show. I'm so sorry."

"Fuck," I groan, searching for a solution since we're moments away. "Okay, tell all the girls to adjust the formation to make up for his absence. Have Becky do her backflip on the left side of the stage where he was supposed to be. Hell, maybe it's better this way since he was the only guy."

"Okay!" they say in unison, taking off.

Turning to Jason, I demand to know, "Why can't things go smoothly?!"

"When it's chaos backstage, the show is great."

"Right. Thank you. Okay. I'll go get her."

I turn for Simone but the door opens and she glides out looking more like a star than ever, hair and makeup perfect. Tiny leather dress that's hot as fuck. Heels that might kill her. Everything is as it should be.

"Katy Perry, watch out," Jason smiles.

She grins at him with the first sign of true excitement shining from her. "Damn straight. Let's do this."

We stand back and let her pass us for the stage, following her. While she waits out of sight, her gaze remains on the floor.

My heart starts pounding like a motherfucker. Jason and I grab hands as we have on many occasions since her album exploded, two songs hitting number one. *Just For Me* stayed there for eleven weeks!

The male announcer's voice booms through the speakers, "And now…Simone. Ross. TAYLOR!!!!!"

Deafening applause and screaming erupts. Simone lifts her head and steps out onto the stage.

I can't stop shifting my feet.

As the dance beat picks up speed, dancers cartwheel and backflip onto stage. Hot pink, red and yellow lights flash over them at the right time. Behind everyone on a huge white screen is a close-up movie of Simone's performance for the people in the back of the auditorium to see her better.

Jason smirks, "See?"

I whisper back to him, "Nobody likes a know-it-all."

* * *

With everyone partying in the larger of the two greenrooms after the show Jason motions for me to follow him. I excuse myself from talking to two men from Simone's label and quietly exit the room.

"What's up?" I smile as I walk up to him.

He's on me so fast I gasp, pulling me behind curtains and slipping his fingers under the hem of my skirt. It's hitching up on my legs and we're so close to everyone I can still pick out some of the conversations. "Jason, stop," I moan, as he bites my neck and growls into my flesh. "Someone might come."

"The only person cumming is gonna be you," he murmurs in my ear as his fingertips slide under my thong. "Fuck, you're wet already."

"With the way you've been watching me, how could I not be?"

"You feel so good,"

I lace my fingers into his hair, moaning, "I'll never be able to show my face around these people again if they find us."

"Bullshit," he growls. "No one gives a fuck. I just have to touch your pussy, Sarah. It's driving me crazy."

He always says he loves seeing me in action when I'm

working. He calls my quick-thinking hot and sometimes throws impossible problems at me to see if I can come up with a solution.

I rub my pelvis against his dark blue jeans, feeling the heat of his bulge and lifting my chin for a kiss. Our tongues slip on each other as he strokes my swelling folds. The ache becomes a throb when he groans in my open lips. Glancing behind us quickly, he pushes the curtain and finds it's got a wall behind it. "Good," he growls, pushing me against it, hiking up my skirt and unzipping his jeans.

"Holy shit, we can't!" I whisper, eyes hooded with lust as he slides two fingers inside me.

Panting in my ear he rasps, "I'm going to fuck you backstage, Sarah. With other people right over there. Can you hear them?"

I moan into his neck and bite him hard. He hisses through his teeth, lifting me up to straddle his narrow hips. One of my feet hooks around his tight ass, the other around his thigh. Rock hard he enters my wetness, hoarsely whispering against my lips, "Fuck you feel so good. So tight. See how hard I am for you right now? How much fucking you in secret is turning me on?"

I moan and accept his tongue while he starts thrusting, stretching my walls as he dives deeper inside me. We're trying to be quiet, keeping our panting as low as we can.

Two voices get louder as footsteps exit the greenroom. Jason freezes and we go very still. Then he starts to move really slowly in and out, as the voices head past us. If whoever that is turned right and looked behind this curtain they'd see us.

The fear heightens my pleasure, I start undulating a little faster.

Jason locks eyes with me, and I can see it's the same for him.

We smile a little at each other as the people stop walking, arguing about food.

"There are a ton of taco places. I want authentic Mexican food."

"No, burgers tonight! I need iron."

The tingles drift through my pussy as Jason keeps fucking me in silence while they're right over there.

"There are burger places within walking distance. The Yard House is right there!"

"Do they have tacos?"

I almost start laughing, but then Jason's cock thickens and he looks at me in such a way that brings me to the brink.

The footsteps pick up again and off they go. "I know for a fact that they have tacos. And french fries."

"Ooooh, I love french fries."

Grinding my hips into Jason, he's deep as he can get.

I throw my head back and explode on his cock.

He locks his teeth onto my neck, his body jerking as he cums inside me, fingers clawing into my ass and thigh.

We move together, drawing the orgasm out until it's over.

Deeply kissing me he carefully sets me down and pulls a tissue from his pocket.

On a low, sex-filled chuckle, I whisper, "You came prepared."

"Excuse the pun."

"Oh, that was terrible!"

He laughs under his breath, "It really was."

40

SARAH

No one has a clue what we just did as we return to the party and separate, socializing once more.

Jason throws me many looks that make me ache for more.

Our sex life is stronger than it was when I first moved in. We experiment. That's part of it. But I think the real reason is we make each other laugh.

Even when we fight — which we do pretty often since we're both strong personalities — the battles often end with us cracking up because someone is being too dramatic or arrogant.

It makes for a very interesting relationship. Grams was right — it's never boring.

And I'm able to travel when Simone needs me. I'm not at all the shows, but I'm at most. A lot of the work I do remotely.

I'm paid a lot better than I used to be, that's for sure.

Simone walks up, glowing and slightly intoxicated. She touches my arm to interrupt my discussion with Mark. Then she calls out to the room, "Everyone, can you all follow me, please? I have a surprise for Sarah."

"What? No! I don't need anything," I blush as she pulls me out of the room toward the stage.

Singing and dancing and pretty drunk as a whole, the dancers follow us.

Usher and Jason are together, talking heatedly about something I can't hear but I know is music-related.

The record executives have their ties loose, their eyes on the dancers.

The engineers aren't with us, so they must have been the tacos vs. burgers people.

Thomas is the only one not with us because he passed out on a couch and is snoring.

Simone walks me to the center of the stage, which is exactly where I *don't* want to be.

"Simone, stop it. You know I hate being in the spotlight."

As if on cue, one ignites, lighting me up and blinding me. I squint against it and look around nervously as the party gathers in a semi-circle so they can all watch.

"What are you doing?" I whisper to her.

She steps back and Jason steps forward into the spotlight. He gets down on one knee and pops open a small velvet box with the most beautiful diamond ring in it. I clamp my hands over my mouth in shock. A hush falls over the stage as tears jump to my eyes.

Jason struggles against his own emotion as he begins, "Sarah Daly, I've never laughed before as much as I do since you came into my life. You drive me crazy, like really fucking crazy..."

Laughter ripples through our audience.

"...and I love it. I love *you* more than I could ever tell you in words. You've made my life real. You give so much and you're so kind and I admire the fuck out of you. I need you. Will you please marry me? Please always stay by my side?"

Tilting my head, I joke, "I don't knooooowwwww..."

He grins, "Maybe think about it?" as people start laughing.

Losing the smile I hold his eyes as tears fall down my cheeks. I struggle against the knot in my throat and whisper, "I would love to marry you, Jason."

He lifts me off the ground and puts the ring on my finger while carrying me as everyone applauds. Then he throws me over his shoulder and spanks my ass while people come over to congratulate us.

"Put me down!" I laugh. "I'm wearing a dress!" He sets me in front of Simone and turns to shake hands with Usher.

She grins like a devil at me. "Teehee."

"So that's why you weren't surprised to see him here."

She shrugs like, *you caught me.*

"But I don't get it, Simone. This was your biggest concert yet. Why let him do this on your special night?"

Her eyes change. "All the times I've been on stage were special. I wanted you to be the star of the show for once."

Unable to speak I give her a tiny nod and mouth, *thank you.*

She hugs me and whispers, "I love you, Sarah."

I can only squeeze her back because the lump in my throat is too huge for little me.

Someone shouts to the engineers to run the music through the speakers. "Let's move the party out here!"

"Fucking best idea ever!" Simone shouts. Off my look she smiles, "Just because I meditate doesn't mean I have to stop swearing." She starts to head off, then looks back over her shoulder to add, "Or drinking."

I laugh and glance over to see my fiancé — oh, my God, Jason just asked me to marry him! — making his way back to me. "It so rare I see you cry," he smirks.

"Well, it won't happen again for a very long time, so..."

His eyebrows are high on his head. "Oh no?"

"Nope."

"You wanna bet when it will?"

I cock my head at him. "What do you mean?"

"Let's bet on the next time you cry."

"That's ridiculous. How would you possibly be able to predict that?"

He takes me by the hand and leads me away from the others. Not out of sight, just far enough that it's a little private.

"Because I know when it'll happen."

"Okay, I'll bite. When is the next time I'll cry, Jason?"

His eyes grow serious as he laces our fingers together and rasps, "When you give birth to our first child."

My lips part as a pang of longing nearly knocks me over.

A child? Me, a mother? I never thought I would have children.

Hell, I never thought I'd have a boyfriend, much less a husband who loved me and who I loved, enough to start a family with.

But Jason Cocker has changed all of that for me.

He's changed...me.

"I can't take that bet, Jason. I'd lose."

He whispers, "I know you would," and bends to kiss me deeply.

I return the kiss, and pull away to whisper against his lips, "You're going to be such a great father."

He smiles and surprises me as tears jump into his eyes. "I want that."

"Me too," I whisper, rising on my tiptoes to throw my arms around him in the biggest hug.

Eight months after our small wedding in Jason's parent's backyard, our son, Max Cocker, is born. And we were both right. I would have lost that bet.

THE END.

COCKER BROTHERS SERIES NOTE

I decided to write bonus chapters for this entire series, scenes that take place years after each book ends so you can experience what happens to these wonderful characters later. For Cocky Roomie, we get to meet their three children. Cocky Cowboy, we get to meet Ben. They're very fun, include more sexy scenes, and can only be accessed by eBook downloads at this time, when you sign up for private club's newsletter. The Kindle app is free for any device, and I also offer Epubs and PDFs.

You can access these through the signup button on my FB Page:

http://facebook.com/authorfaleenahopkins

Enjoy!
Xx, Faleena Hopkins

TO GET IN TOUCH:

www. AuthorFaleenaHopkins.com

http://facebook.com/authorfaleenahopkins
(mailing list link is there under: Signup)

Twitter and Instagram: @faleenahopkins

Pinterest: FaleenaMHopkins
(there is a board dedicated to this series)

To learn more about my acting/filmmaking career:
http://imdb.me/faleenahopkins

BY FALEENA HOPKINS

Cocky Roomie
Cocky Biker
Cocky Cowboy
Cocky Romantic
(Senator and Soldier, en route)

You Don't Know Me

Anything For You Series:
Changing For You
Reaching For You
Searching For You

Werewolves Of Chicago: Curragh
Werewolves Of Chicago: Howard
Werewolves Of Chicago: Xavier

Werewolves Of New York: Nathaniel
Werewolves Of New York: Eli
Werewolves Of New York: Darik
Werewolves Of New York: Dontae

Fire Nectar Vampires: The Choice
Fire Nectar Vampires: The Elders

Faleena Hopkins

ABOUT THE AUTHOR

Faleena Hopkins published her first novel in May of 2013 and due to the warm reception of her stories, was able to quit her day-job as a professional portrait photographer by September of that year to write full time.

A California native and a Los Angeles resident for twenty-three years, she moved to Atlanta, GA in December 2015 to write love stories and prepare filming for her first independent feature film. This is where the Cocker Brothers series was inspired.

Also an actress for over twenty years, her work has been praised in reviews by the Los Angeles Times, Variety and Hollywood Reporter and she intends to direct and star in her first movie, to keep pushing the boundaries of what people say she can and cannot do.

The bracelet she wears every day bears the engraving: *She believed she could so she did.* Inspiring others to follow their dreams is a big part of her passion and she regularly helps authors self-publish their way to success by sharing how she was able to get where she is, and the mistakes she navigated along the way.